psylicon
beach

300

Also by Philip Gross:

Plex
Transformer
The Wind Gate

Also in Scholastic Press:

Love Lessons
David Belbin

Criss Cross
Susan Gates

Out of the Mouths of Babes
Dennis Hamley

Unquiet Spirits
K. M. Peyton

Flying Upside Down
Malcolm Rose

Technofear
Laurence Staig

psylicon beach

Philip Gross

SCHOLASTIC
PRESS

Scholastic Children's Books,
Commonwealth House, 1-19 New Oxford Street,
London WC1A 1NU, UK
a division of Scholastic Ltd
London ~ New York ~ Toronto ~ Sydney ~ Auckland

First published in the UK by Scholastic Ltd, 1998

ISBN 0 590 19808 4

Typeset by DP Photosetting, Aylesbury, Bucks.
Printed by Cox and Wyman Ltd, Reading, Berks.

10 9 8 7 6 5 4 3 2 1

Contents

BeMovie   1

Governor: *Duckhead's Story*   41

Sand Golem   75

Creeper: *Cazzie's Story*   87

Wildcatting   121

The Big One   149

BeMovie

1.

The alligator wasn't happy in the swimming pool.

The Major-Domo wasn't happy, either. His mirror-spangled waistcoat was shimmering with rage. This time of day it was Happy Hour in the holiday time-shares and the Sherbet Fountain's shady colonnades should have been full of guests, sipping long thin drinks, their long pale faces gazing out on the court-yard, tinkling a small bell now and then to call a slave. But there was no one. One sight of the alligator and they'd bolted. "So they'll be in the bar," I said to the M-D. "What's the problem?" He'd been a barman himself before he got the plum job at the Sherbet Fountain. He was nobody's fool.

"*What's the problem?*" he said. "The way they're downing those speedy ginseng sips, each glass they're getting edgier, more hyper. Making calls to the company, to their lawyers." That's why he'd sent for me. Good old Scip, always equal to the situation. For a price. I was sizing this Situation up now, wondering what the price might be.

It was only a minor alligator compared to some of

the big guys I meet out in the Creek. The guests, who never looked outside their pleasure domes, might consider it quite big. All the better if they did. The thing must have waddled its way across the Boulevard, out of the moat at Arthurian World. Why it took it into its mind to cross hot tarmac in the middle of the day I couldn't guess ... unless it was the M-D over there who set it off in our direction. The Sherbet Fountain was their nearest competition, after all.

The poor beast didn't look well to me. It lay in the deep end with its six legs splayed. The extra legs, run-of-the-mill mutations from the toxins in the Creek, made it look like a stretch-limo in some quaint last-millennium film. Its tail gave occasional shudders. My guess was it had OD'd on the chemicals they put in the pools – you know, to stop them from turning to steam in the heat. Or was it the sea-spray perfume they splash in, to go with the synthesized sound of breakers pounding on the shore? That was what the guests still looked for, fooled by the word *Beach* or by the walkaround 3-D brochures they saw in the city or wherever people come from when they aren't on holiday. I thought of the old-world paint-picture I salvaged once, out in the shallows. Most of it had rotted but you could still make out waves on a big wide sea, the kind of sea there used to be before the warming when the one big tide came in and stayed. In this picture, the waves were breaking into smoke with blue-white horses rearing out of them, manes blowing back in the wind. Just a horse in a field was strange enough these days, and almost certainly synthetic. White horses in the sea was weird and wild.

"Well?" said the M-D.

"Pretty big," I said, playing it canny. He looked at me sideways. He's nobody's fool, like I said. The alligator clacked its jaws, more of a yawn than a snap. I shrugged. "No bother. It'll have snuffed it by teatime. No sense in annoying it while it's dying."

"Teatime?" He shook his head. "By teatime they'll have packed their bags and gone. They'll be in Arthurian World or the Kubla Khan. Or shuttling back to the city, filing suits for breach of contract. We're in the sump." He screwed his plum-coloured fez down tighter on his head; a little wave of sweat squeezed out. "Our only chance," he said, "is turn the Situation into Entertainment."

I looked at him. He hadn't mentioned terms yet. This could be worth my while after all.

"We need a bit of a show," he said. "Of course I thought of you."

He's OK, is the M-D, perfectly OK as trained toadies go. Under the fancy dress and smooth talk you can see him watching you, cool as a solar-powered fridge. Peaktime Timeshares Corporation shipped him in from some small country they bought up on the cheap, and put him through their Courtesy Intensive till courtesy dripped from the tips of his moustache. But under all that there was a part of him that looked at me and thought: *there but for the grace of the Corporation, go I...*

"A loincloth," he said. "We'll provide a loincloth and a spear."

I said a word they hadn't taught him at courtesy school.

"Don't push your luck," he said, eyes narrowing all of a sudden. "There's a hundred other trashtypes like you out there in the Outer Lots."

"Ah, but this is a water job," I said. "Most of them won't touch the stuff... Anyway," I smiled, "you trust me."

"Up to a point," he said.

"Thinking of which," I said, "did you say *spear*? You mean, a pointed stick?"

He bared his teeth as if pretending this was all a joke. "More of a harpoon. We've got one left over from the Last Whale Day parade. Very sharp, and there's a barbed bit at the end. You can keep your own knife." I can't have looked mega-convinced. "You said it yourself: the thing's half dead already," he said. "And Ezekiel will have the sonic stunner, just in case."

"Thanks. What about my eardrums?"

"It won't be necessary, of course. An insurance policy, is all. Nobody wants you eaten. We pride ourselves on tasteful entertainment at the Sherbet Fountain. This isn't the Zoo."

"What terms?" I said.

"Free pass for the bar tonight. You can do what deals you like. Discreetly. And a dash of credit – let's say twenty-five bits? – in your Small Change account." He had me there. Without a fixed address, or not an official one, the system won't charge an account – that means you've got no credit, anywhere – so mine was *c/o* Sherbet Fountain Timeshare. As long as it suited them. Fair enough. Twenty-five. It was quite a small alligator.

"OK, OK, shake on it," I said.

I cut down to the beach, to give him an hour to coax the punters back to the pool. Upwind, a smell of barbecued sheep substitute wafted down from the Kubla Khan. Half their guests were outdoors, crouched in their pseudo-leather yurts, their nomad tents. The Kubla Khan experience is that you get to be the barbarian hordes who swept in off the steppe to ravage Europe, way back when. The Pleasure Dome wavered slightly in the heat haze, like a transmission starting to break up on an ancient sky-TV screen.

I kept close to the small chalk cliff at the high tide mark, partly for shade, partly from habit. There's always surveillance from the watchtowers round the perimeter fence. You never know when it might come in useful, not to have them knowing where you are.

Out in the open a small bunch of kids was scavenging, in loose rags, barefoot and bent double, in the stones.

"Hey, Scip!" one called, and the others looked up, sharp-eyed, from under their makeshift sunshades. "Anything doing?"

"Usual nothings," I shrugged. They took a step towards me, not a serious move, just establishing their stakehold on this bit of beach. Probably found a cache of crude last-century silicon chips. Two a penny, of course – how else did the place get its name? – but they could string them into necklets for the tourists. Petty stuff, not my kind of business. As I walked past they relaxed. At twenty paces I turned round and called back, "And it's Scipio to you."

I ducked through the rusted chain-link that marked the start of the Pollution Danger zone. Down in the jungleweed I pulled my boat out of hiding, with my bag of bargain goodies untouched inside. A couple of glitter-discs from some ancient music system, a wristband with a round face on it and some numbers, and a pair of turn-of-the-millennium mirrored eye-shades. Only trinkets, not serious antiquities, but still worth good cred if you can spot your customer, your serious nostalgia freak. A different class of junk, at any rate, from the stuff the gang on the beach could grub for. You get these things by diving – deep – and you have to know where. You have to dare.

When I got back to the Sherbet Fountain, the M-D

had fixed me a costume. "Put this on," he said. It was a wig, yellow, shoulder-length. Barbarian chic. "You've got to have something." He nodded at my smooth scalp and wrinkled his nose. I don't remember when my hair went – some time after I started diving in the Grey Stacks. No one knows what kind of toxins they've got leaking from the drowned works there. Hair? I'm more streamlined without it. Still, a blond wig... He looked me up and down. "Can't have our customers thinking it's a freak show," he said in his Courtesy Intensive voice.

Now for the Situation. I lowered myself into the sea-spray-scented water and pushed off from the side, harpoon in hand. In the deep end the alligator stirred. It hadn't shifted much but there was something in the way it twitched that pressed a warning bleeper in my gut. It was meant to be snuffing it slowly, like things naturally slow down and die from poisons in the wild. Its tail tip flicked, just once, and cruised the body round towards me. The snout broke water and behind that, lining up, the eyes. It started treading water, inching forward. All round, there was a soft but many-throated sigh.

A ring of faces, mouths hung open. All the guests were there. Not just the Sherbet Fountain's but a lot from the other timeshares, too. The M-D had been advertising this little floorshow, and quickly. No, he couldn't have got word round that quickly. Not unless he'd billed the whole show in advance.

The alligator jiggled forward, left-right, like a thing on elastic ready to be fired. It looked a whole lot livelier than anything that sick could be. Unless. . .

"Hey, wait a minute. . ." I said.

The Major-Domo's face smiled down from the poolside, perfectly impassive, and suddenly it all made sense to me. A man like him, bar-trained, knows how to mix a cocktail. The alligator I saw earlier hadn't been sick, just wallowing in a happy, druggy sleep. That's why they'd sent me away for an hour, to give it time to wake up. Probably it had whatever a hangover feels like in a dark small reptile brain. It was twitchy and tetchy and easily riled.

"No way. . ." I said, and as I grabbed at the metal steps I saw that, in one thing at least, the M-D was good as his word. Ezekiel, two-metres square in tuxedos, was there with the stun-gun. In a movement too slight for the crowd to notice, he twitched the barrel – not at the alligator but at me. *You*, his eyes said, *stay right there*. Then the water frothed and I wrenched myself sideways, bunching my legs up and kicking off just as the alligator's bow-wave hit me. Its jaws clanged shut on the rungs of the steps. With a yank of its head it wrenched them out of the concrete, tossed them about a bit, then motored round to face me.

Fifty faces leaned towards us, straining forward off

their seats. Their grins weren't smiles now, they were blood lust, and I knew that this was what they'd booked for, weeks ago. A simulated trailer for this scene had probably been beamed to the comfort of their living-rooms, as they planned for a hard year of leisure ahead.

Only one wasn't craning and gaping; that was why he caught my eye. With the sudden and useless clarity they say people get in the instant before death, I saw how out of all the hundreds just this one kid, no older than me, was lounging back, bored. He wasn't even looking; he was staring into his Pineapple Meltdown cocktail as if there was an especially interesting insect drowning in it. But I knew him. Ivo Maccaby.

Savage, that's what the film was called. Plane-crashed on a desert island, everybody else dead, this kid from a really upstream paleface family goes back to nature, goes wild and... Yes, there was a scene in a swamp pool. With an alligator. And the kid who played the kid, the billion-dollar brat, was Ivo Maccaby. No wonder he was behaving like he'd seen it all before.

The alligator made its rush, its two eyes coming at me with a look that made me think of the M-D. Flattening against the side, I jabbed the harpoon straight at one eyeball, a risk (a tiny target in a lot of armour) but it must have come close enough for instinct to take over, and the alligator jerked its head aside. As it came swerving round for a clear run, I thought: *of course, the M-D!* He was just above me now, one steel-tipped sandal poised in case I grabbed the edge and started to climb out. I knew this was all in a day's work to him, showbiz. But all of a sudden I began to take it personally.

My left hand on the side, I swiped out with the harpoon in my right. It didn't catch the M-D cleanly; the barb of it caught in his pantaloon trousers and I yanked, with both hands, as hard as I could. And his top-heavy bulk came towards me, right over the edge.

Confused by the movement, the alligator hesitated, then it launched itself again. With that behind me and the M-D in free fall above, I made a decision, or my instincts made it for me: not to get out of the way. The man's weight caught me like a plunger, thudding me down, two metres underwater, just as the alligator hit the spot, and for a minute the two of them were tangling up above me, clouds of foam and bubbles laced with blood. Then I came up straight under them, harpoon tip first, up and into the alligator's soft bits, and before it knew it I'd pushed off the side with both feet and the long bag of its belly unzipped in a smoky burst of guts – all over me, it's true, but would you care?

There were hands reaching down now and hauling me out. I went sprawling on the tiles like a beached fish. All around was cheering, maybe, or a mingled roar of disappointment and applause. Ezekiel was fishing for the M-D, bleeding, yes, but not too cut up, at a glance. As soon as he had his boss out, he'd attend to me. Being attended to by Ezekiel is a famous way to go. I tried to get up on my feet, slipped, cracked down on one kneecap, tried again. . .

Then he was leaning down, helping me up. The brat-star Ivo Maccaby. To be honest, I hated his films. Right now, though, he was a descending angel.

"My friend!" he announced to the rest of the crowd, in a voice an octave lower than the voice he had on film. "My friend. My alter ego. This boy dines with me."

"Thanks," I said, back at his table. A waiter had tactfully appeared with a bath-sheet and draped it on my shoulders, but Ivo had waved him away. The white towelling was smudging brown and pink now – alligator guts and blood. Ivo gave me an approving look.

"Wild," he said. "Now *that* was savage."

"You did it neater in the film."

His broad grin froze and darkened. "Well," he shook his head, "depending what you mean by *me*. . ."

Suddenly his glance went up behind my shoulders; grabbing a squat cut-glass pepperpot he hurled it, hard. There was a yelp, and a man with a hand-held 3-D camcorder staggered back, tripped on the groaning mass of the M-D, scrambled to his feet and was off at a run.

"Damn," Ivo said. "That's another bit gone. . ." He must have seen me frown. "Don't ask," he said. "Don't ask, because I'm going to tell you anyway. But first we eat." He glanced at the menu. "Wouldn't you know it? Special of the day is alligator steak."

2.

Coming at Psylicon Beach from the sea, the first thing you notice is... Hold it, *nobody* comes to the Beach from the sea. Unless you count me, that is, Scipio, and everyone knows *I'm* nobody.

But if you did come up the Creek, nosing up it as it narrows from the mile-wide Gulf of London, if you ducked past the alarm-buoys and the signs flashing DANGER: TOXIC ZONE, if you edged your way in through the concrete reefs of the Grey Stacks where a jagged tip of a corroded pylon could open up your boat neat as gutting a fish, then you'd come round the corner and catch your first sight of . . . well, not much at all.

You'd see some trees, that's true – a bit too square and sudden to be natural – at the head of the Creek. Above and around, it's bare-bones country, where the grass has scorched and flash floods stripped the soil from chalk hills. Around this oasis, you might notice the fence and the watch towers – cunningly screened from the timeshares on the inside, but on full view for outsiders looking in. Like me. With the sun at the right angle you might catch a glint of penthouse glass, or the pseudo-gilding of a dome. From that point in it's wonderland, it's the holiday you've been dying for, it's anything you can imagine, it's the junkshop of dreams that is Psylicon Beach.

The Choice is Yours! This is the walk-round virtual brochures speaking. *This year, will it be the harsh heroic world of First Dark Age England? Will it be the scented pleasures of the mystic East?* Glimpse of the Sherbet Fountain on a good day, with your own Sheherezade at every café table, telling you stories as if her life depended on it? Or the knights of Arthurian World who'll challenge you to joust, and always let you win? In the background, maybe, the less said the better, there are the basalt columns and sand-whittled sphinxes of the Necropolitan Club. There's no accounting for the weirdos who hang round Nefertiti's Tomb.

It's not all ancient. Take a stroll through the endless, endlessly-receding aisles of stalls and boutiques in the 20th Century Nostalgia street market, every kind of last-millennium style aid from 1920s feather boas, through the Sixties and punk, rave, techno, retro, to the revolutionary New Normal fashions of the end. All this to appropriate music, filtered through the gentle swish of sprinklers keeping the flowerbeds moist, the grass green, and the illusion (that's what they pay for) that there's still such a thing as rain.

What the brochures won't show is the Outer Lots, with the bald foundations or half-finished walls the speculators started in boom time, when it looked as if Psylicon Beach might be big, big, BIG. Empty, you'd say. Abandoned. Derelict. You might not see — because they're good at not being seen too often – the stray cats and stray kids who have their homes out there, their lairs, their secret beats.

Zoom in on the Sherbet Fountain timeshare, past the heavy door guards disguised as eunuchs and genies, up the wide staircase that's keeping up the appearance of marble today, since Illusion Control has just had a service and is up and running for another year. (Without that, you'd see ... who knows? Probably bare concrete, a hundred years the worse for wear.) At the top of the stairs the Major-Domo, slightly bandaged, greets you by name, even if you are a total stranger, and can grease you to an exclusive table, if you can buzz for a little extra credit to appear mysteriously in his tips account.

Or you might glide into the Caravanserai bar, with fractal-patterned ceiling arches crowding in like a forest, in a maze of mirrors. Here in a dim corner (or is it that dim corner over there, and this one's a reflection, and that one, and that?) you might see two young types talking at a table. One brushes their bald head awkwardly, suddenly realizing that the wig is out in the pool, floating like a blond jellyfish. The other leans back, with that expensive kind of chuckle only available to people who can pay for privacy and space. He wears a platinum silk-look baggy blouse, in the house style, open at the neck where he's got a stud implanted just in the place that forms a triangle with the end nubs of his collar bones. It's very tasteful and expensive-looking, some sort of hypo-allergenic space metal from its matt glint, and it flashes an "I" at certain angles of the virtual candlelight.

"Who are you, anyway?" said Ivo. As if to water down the question, he topped up my glass with something opalescent: *Liquid Moon*, the bottle said.

"I'm in business." You can't be too cautious. The richer they are, the less they understand. "In a small way. Old things."

"Trashtypes. That's what the Major-Domo calls you and your friends." If I had eyebrows I'd have raised them at that last word. Maybe rich kids do have friends . . . though from what I see, it seems unlikely. But Ivo was leaning forwards, chin almost resting on his Liquid Moon. "What's it like, being you?"

I shrugged. "It's a life."

He frowned suddenly. "Don't fence with me," he said. "I'm asking you questions. These old things of yours. . . What you *do*?"

"OK. . ." Maybe truth was the commodity he wanted. Even in a place like this, some do. "I get them from out in the Creek."

"Underwater? You're a diver? Is that what they all do?"

"Them? They duck-dive in the shallows, one or two of them. Small fry. You want a diver, I'm the one."

He let his breath out slowly. "Hey," he said. "That's massive." He stared into his Moon. "What's out there . . . out where no one's meant to go?"

He wanted something. What, I couldn't tell, but he wanted it enough, I guessed, to pay. I tapped my nose. "Trade secret," I said, then, to soften the bargaining with a little joke: "If I told you, you might make a film of it."

Smash. His hand made a fist and punched his glass right off the table. It shattered and the drink lay quivering on its own like mercury across the floor. A waiter glanced once, and didn't come over. With guests like Ivo the damage is charged to the bill and, for an extra small charge, nothing said.

"Get this straight," Ivo whispered. "I don't make films."

"I've seen dozens," I lied. "They were great." But Ivo was on his feet. For a moment I thought he was going to storm out and leave me there, no business done. But he beckoned, sharply.

"You think you know what's what, eh?" His voice

was dangerous. "Just because you're out there in the garbage, you think you know it all."

"Not me," I said hastily. "Not me. You want to tell me?"

"Maybe I do," he said. "Maybe we'll get on better than you think. Maybe there's something you can tell me, too." The lift was waiting for us; as it sensed our warmth, it opened. Ivo pushed me in. As he punched the Up button, the sheet-plastic walls flickered a little with the ghosts of clouds and snow-capped land- scapes. Somewhere in Illusion Control the Magic Carpet chip was on the blink again.

Ivo's eyes flickered round the corners of the lift. He clapped a hand over a small pane of darkened glass whose purpose wasn't clear. "Bugs," he said. "Everywhere. Wait till we get to my room. Then we can talk for real."

He'd been sprawling for an hour, arms and legs splayed, in his heated vibro-nest. He ignored me. I crouched on the floor, waiting for the most expensive chair I'd ever seen to massage the little tensions out of his back and shoulders. Suddenly he yawned. "Let's do a game." He reached down a pocket console with more buttons than I'd ever seen, and zapped up a gestalt field wide as the apartment. There was that quivering look to the air, like a heat haze, as all its particles waited to be organized into . . . what?

"Banzai!" A robo-commando smashed through the wall, which was suddenly a third-floor window; twisted like a cat and landed running, sub-machine gun blazing, coming straight at us. Ivo hit the triggers and a burst of fire from nowhere scythed the robo-guy in half, so that the legs came on a few paces under their own momentum before buckling at the knees.

There's something comforting about a good shoot-'em-up game. I guess it's like the feeling people used to have about the seasons, when they had them. Even if you lived in the middle of a city you would get that feeling in the air, spring or whatever, and you'd feel that nothing really changes, deep down. I've seen bits of some really ancient video games, museum pieces, the originals with glass screens. The same all-out assault, the bad guys coming at you – these days you get to watch it in more detail, from all sides, and they really do come at you, that's all.

As the commando's top half hit the ground, his visor cracked back and there was something weirdly familiar about the glimpse of face inside. I didn't look too close. Ivo zapped up the level by two or three notches, and suddenly there were assailants coming out of every crevice. He tossed me a spare trigger pad, as a mutant gorilla-clone wrestler dropped from the scaffolding right at the edge of the illusion field, so he seemed to have come from the lampshade. I was slower than Ivo – he'd been playing this, I guessed, most days for years. But I unzipped the apeman neatly, and then it was happening so quickly that I didn't ponder much for quite a while. It was more fun, let's be honest, than what I'd been expecting: a whole evening's re-runs of the catalogue of Ivo films.

Then I was bored. I glanced sideways at Ivo, who was staring at the battle, thin-lipped, with unblinking eyes. The moment I let go my trigger pad the program knew, so all the things converged on him. We'd moved on from simple human-style combatants an hour ago; there were centaurs and insect-men and bat-people swooping from the skies now or erupting from the earth. As I watched, the same creepy feeling I'd had with the first commando filtered back and stayed. Each of the assailants, whatever monstrous claws or wings or fins, had a human face, the same face – Ivo's own.

With a starburst of fire he cleared the street and threw the trigger down. The scene began to fade. "What's up?" he said. "Can't stand the pace?"

"Ivo," I said, "I don't like the feel of it. I mean ... those guys out there, they're *you.*"

"Me?" He jerked forward towards me. "How do you know who *me* is, trashtype? How do I know, or anyone? The corporation, they've got bits of me, that's all."

That rang a bell. "What did you mean," I said, "down there in the bar: '*that's another bit gone...*'? It was that guy with the camcorder, wasn't it?"

"Ever heard of the tribe," he said, "who thought that every time a tourist pointed a camera at them they stole part of their soul? Dead primitive, huh? And that was just with old-world photographs." He flicked up the field for an instant, running on the lowest level, so a fairly minor warrior came in full view, lumbering towards him. It was in Barbarian kit, mainly a loincloth, with blond hair that could have been cut with the aid of its only weapon, a knife. No mistake, it was Ivo from *Savage*.

He let it get to point-blank distance, slowly, then blew it apart with something meant for missile bunkers, not for men. The gestalt field went down, but the bits of the corpse twitched on for a minute before the force that organized them into being gave out. There was no blood on the carpet. Ivo laughed.

"Hell, you're angry," I said. "What's he – I mean, you – I mean, that thing ever done to you?"

Ivo slumped back in the vibro-nest and gave his back a pummel. "OK," he said. "You really want to know?"

It was around the time the contract for the second film came up he discovered they'd stolen his soul.

"I didn't know," he said again. "I mean, your own folks. . ." For a second he was just the kid he'd once been – tough enough to have adventures but still sort of vulnerable.

"Your folks?" I said. "But they're so nice."

Mr and Mrs Niceguy, that was Ivo's mother and father. They were famous for it – a real *couple* with family values and old-fashioned ways. After the films, they began to celebrate their wedding anniversary with little meals for two where the press could happen by. Later there were invites issued, all the press and corporation moguls, the whole restaurant booked for the night.

Some cynics whispered it was just a style thing, an attempt to revive New Normal fashions, a deal with some wholesaler who had a warehouse of the gear stashed somewhere. But the Maccaby family was a small time-capsule in itself, a micro-theme-park that more and more people seemed to want to visit. And no one could deny the fact that they were nice.

Plenty of families take home videos, always did. And so did the Maccaby family. As the technology got smarter, they upgraded. So the picture of cute little Ivo was captured from more and more angles; it was digitized and stored. "The database," growled Ivo. "They had it on-line, more or less, from the time I could walk." So it grew, the database did, with Ivo; rather faster than Ivo, in fact, because you didn't need much of a program to edit, sample, change an angle, animate a different frame or two. It might have been *Savage* that made the difference, finally. The database called Ivo came of age.

There was this scene where he had to do a hundred-metre dive from a cliff and there was no way Ivo, or anyone but a purpose-built bio-clone could do that. Besides, he was valuable already. So a bit of quick programming work and audiences saw Ivo Maccaby walk to the edge of the cliff, no jump-cuts, no join visible, and step off the edge into free fall and a perfect dive. He was virtually flying. And it all took off, as you might say, from there.

Ivo Maccaby was big bucks. He was business. "I was handling it fine," said Ivo. "Then all of a sudden they flew this shrink in."

"We're worried about you, son," said his father, and why not have a chat with this nice Dr Spellman, which he did. He was bored, was Ivo, and this doctor woman sat on her swivel chair with her legs tucked up, the kind of long legs young Ivo was starting to notice, so he talked to her, about this and that and what it felt like being Ivo, for day after day. He didn't know, not then, that this was all being taped, filmed, fed into the database.

"You've changed," said his mother, in the family sessions, and her eyes began to brim with tears. "We feel we're losing you," his mother said. "Our little baby..." Dr Spellman did batteries of tests and psychometric readings, biorhythms, charts. Everything about Ivo that could be measured, was. Dr Spellman ("Call me Andromache," she was saying by this time.

"Trust me.") prescribed exercise: running, swimming, an assault course, unarmed combat. All recorded, stored for future reference. Digitized, patented, copyrighted.

Still, it came as a shock, after months of Dr S's tucked-up legs and nice attentive eyes, when she summoned his parents in. They sat side by side on the sofa, sort of solemn, as if they knew in advance that this week's episode was titled THE BAD NEWS.

"I have come to the conclusion," said Dr Spellman, "that the pressures of this life could be too much for him. He needs a holiday."

The first of the timeshares they put him in was luxury. "Not," said Ivo, "begging your pardon, like this dump."

"Don't apologize," I said. "I didn't build it."

It was when he had got bored, moved on, got bored, made himself a nuisance, and been moved on for the third or fourth time that it happened. *The Return of the Savage* came out. It was almost by chance the morning newstext told him it was showing in the big-screen bar: the brand new Ivo Maccaby film. This was the first Ivo Maccaby had heard about it. He called his parents, with the screen of the video phone turned off so they wouldn't see him pale and trembling. "Hi there, Momsy," he said, as casually as he could. "What's new?"

"Nothing," she said. "Nothing." And that's when he

knew they'd taken something that you might call his soul.

Crouched in the back row of the big-screen bar that night he was rigid, holding on to the hope that it might just be an actor, an amazing lookalike. But no: he began to spot small gestures, things he hardly knew he did, until he thought back to Dr Spellman's sessions and thought: *yes, I did that then*. Just as the credits rolled, him at the top of the billing, Ivo Maccaby erupted.

They could have hushed it up, easy, they could have paid for the smashed chairs, broken glasses, even the injuries to hotel staff, with one split second of *The Return of the Savage*'s takings. But just by bad luck there was this local press-hound there. He got the interview: Ivo, blind drunk on shock and rage, spilling the beans on the world's top favourite Normal family. What a scoop.

It never reached the world, of course. It took a small bite out of profits and the newshound in question hasn't been heard of again, but still, the interview never appeared. And when some fans who'd heard a rumour turned up at the timeshare, Ivo wasn't there, and an unfortunate error had wiped the central booking data. Ivo's leisure advisers had advised, advised most strongly, that he move on. The armoured limo that came for him had locks on the doors. He moved on.

"Not too sure about the next bit." Ivo looked at me, weary. "That's when I discovered Liquid Moon, for one thing. And they moved me so often. Just to keep my mind off things, they said. Must be three, four years – how d'you keep count? And I've seen a thing or two on the way..."

His eyes went glazed a moment, as if he'd flicked the screen back on, in some private way I couldn't see or hear.

"Get me out of this place," he said suddenly. "Just for an evening. A night. I'll pay you anything you like. Just get me out of here."

3.

"I don't know why I'm doing this." I was whispering from habit, though I knew if they were really scanning for us then a heartbeat was enough. We short-cut through the Perfumed Garden. It had shut down for the night, so there was no smell but a faint scorched smell of a micro-connection shortcircuiting somewhere in the leaves which would not be in rustling mode till morning.

Over in the shadows there were little pantings and the glass gazebo shuddered slightly. I didn't need infrared scanners to recognize the outline of the Major-Domo ... and the girl who did the Seven Veils routine. This was better than I'd have dared hope for. Not only an item of gossip worth good cred from several people's accounts, but he was sure to have bribed surveillance to look the other way. Still, we had to move quickly. We vaulted the low wall where the virtual peacocks strutted in the day, and we slipped down a slope to the outer rim of real but scrawny trees. I could see the perimeter fence, skilfully veiled from both the timeshare and the passing punter's eyes. It was dark now, no moon up yet, and the only light was a blue-white glow from behind a knoll on the perimeter, behind or underneath it, as if it came from underground.

"Head for that," I pointed. "The GIGO."

"What?" said Ivo.

"Garbage In Garbage Out," I whispered. "Keep your head down. Run." Just this side of the mound I threw myself flat and listened. "Hear that?"

Ivo frowned. "My heart," he said.

"The conveyor's working. Must be a truck due. We're in luck." I kept low, wriggling round the contour of the mound so we wouldn't present a profile to the scanners that would certainly be sweeping. After a while my fingers found what I was after: a steel grille set neatly in the dust. It was loose, as I knew it would be; I had been in and out this way before.

From under it came a grinding and a sound like clanking chains.

"What now?" said Ivo.

"We wait. It's down to timing." So we lay on our backs on the low knoll and waited. I could have lain there staring, just listing the meaningless words — Ursa Minor, Pleiades, Cassiopeia — I'd once found printed on two clear plastic discs I'd fished out on a difficult museum dive. *Planisphere*, it said round the rim. It was weeks before I realized what was on them: if you turned one disk beneath the other your view of the stars changed, just like the real sky.

At first Ivo was twitchy. Every now and then there was a screech or a howl from the Zoo compound, not quite animal or human; they were meant to double-bolt the doors when they had all-night parties, but there were rumours of break-outs. Each time Ivo winced. He glanced at the stars but they weren't what he wanted. He gazed at the Creek.

"Why am I doing this?" I said, more to myself than Ivo.

"Money. Don't act dumb."

"Dumb? I can't use your money." He made a little scoffing sound. I rolled over to face him. "Listen," I said. "Every tip I get the timeshare sees. They're on-line to the cred computer. And they take their cut. They aren't too keen on private deals." Ivo was quiet for a moment, lost in wonder either at the stars or the thought of life without a proper charge account. I didn't say: "If it's money I'm after, you're more use to me in this place than out of it." Why rub it in? "Anyway," I said. "What would I do with it?"

He shrugged. "Anything. Leave here, for a start."

"I could walk out the front gate right now," I said. "Can you?" There was no reply to that. What else were we doing creeping like mega-rats round the garbage chute?

"Well, then? Why *are* you doing it?"

"You'll have stories. I collect them." Information.

That's what puts me ahead of the others, with their nano-sec attention spans. But Ivo shook his head and went on gazing at the Creek.

The moon was up behind the Grey Stacks. Just the tips of them broke surface, barbs of black against the moon-pale sky.

"Got to get there." Ivo's voice was thin and strange.

"It's pretty ugly out there," I said.

"But it's real..." His voice was faint, like poor reception on a broadcast. "...never really been ... *out*. You know what I mean?"

"Don't kid yourself," I said. "If it's real it's ugly. You were better off back there."

"Toxic..." he said, in a wondering sort of voice.

"Sure," I shrugged. "You got allergies?"

"Thousands," he said, proudly. I forget: if you're rich then it's good to be sensitive. It explains why you have to have things done for you. Why you have to be protected. "My room at the timeshare, it gets sterilized three times a day. Parents' orders..." His voice went faraway again. "Some nights ... I used to dream of TOXIC. Just the word at first, then I saw pictures of a sea like this, but weird colours, purple, brown and green..."

"Fish die out there," I said. "People's hair falls out. You want that? God knows what else it's done to me. Ivo, how old do you think I am?"

He squinted at me. "Dunno... Thirteen, maybe?"

"And how long do you think I've been it?" I said. And I meant it. I've got no idea. I used to count the years once, then I lost count and after that it just went on for ever. Ivo didn't reply. "Besides which," I said, "what's so great about real?"

"Take me there," he said. "Quickly."

"Not tonight," I said. "Plenty of time for that."

"What if there isn't?"

Just then, beyond the fence, was a very low rumble. A truck. "Hush," I said. "Listen. When I make a move, you follow." And I prised the grille up from the ground.

There was a grinding hum somewhere down in the tunnel; that would be the outer doors. Then a deeper rumble as the truck backed in. I eased my body through the grille, down to my armpits, and let my feet dangle. "Quick!" I hissed, and Ivo wriggled down beside me. For a moment we were just our top thirds, like the robo-commando he had mown down in the game. In the darkness beneath us, something long and heavy trundled just below our feet.

"Drop," I said. I dropped. He didn't; his nerve failed. I hit the soft mound of garbage in the open-topped container and started to slither, but I grabbed at Ivo's foot and yanked. With a small yelp, he came through the hatch and squelched beside me. For a minute there was a smell so horrible it grabbed your throat like being strangled from the inside. Ivo vomited beside me. Such a waste of Liquid Moon.

Then the darkness was lightening. Our container trundled out of its tunnel and into the glare of arc lights. Ivo's head came up to look. I pushed it down. There was a loud metallic clang and I caught a glimpse of the garbage truck driver standing by his half-a-football-pitch-length of armoured steel. Why armoured, you might ask? The stuff only gets dumped on landfill mountains up in the hinterland where whole towns, whole tent-cities of scavengers wait. Ah yes, but we wouldn't want the guests to see it happen here.

The driver slammed the back hatch open. It was Duckhead. This might be luck or not, depending. Steel grabs lowered and clamped the container in front of us, and its contents slowly avalanched into the transport truck. It sounded like Ivo had, vomiting, but fifty times louder, and went on for fifty times as long.

The cart in front banged back down and ours nudged forwards. Ivo yelped as the grab-arms brought their awful bearhug down round us. "Jump first," I yelled, "before you're buried." And we jumped, just as the container started tilting; we launched ourselves into the yawning darkness of the garbage truck.

"Good Golly, what's this?" A head and shoulders peered in as the avalanche settled. I could see the guy's ancient Elvis Presley hairstyle even in silhouette. "Ratkids!"

"Duckhead, it's me, Scip," I yelled. "Got some goods for you. Let's deal!" But Duckhead didn't answer. He tilted his hairstyle, as if thinking. Then he slammed the back hatch shut.

There was a jolt, and the truck pulled off slowly. Then it stopped. There was the clunk of another lever and an awful slushy grinding, very near. Somewhere under the garbage, the metal-toothed compactor screw started turning, so we felt the garbage sucking around our feet. "Duckhead!" I screamed and hammered on the truck wall.

Clunk. The grinder stopped. There was a creak and a half-inch of light. "I hear you, ratboy," Duckhead called in. "Just so you know who's calling the shots. I think you said: 'let's deal'?"

"Got a rich kid," I said. "Mega-mega-rich. Right here beside me. Half a metre from that screw."

Duckhead thought for a moment. "Uh-huh," he said. "Nah. Hostage taking's not my scene." There was a pause. "If he's so rich," said Duckhead, "what's he doing in the garbage?"

"Get us out and I'll tell you."

Duckhead slowly shook his head – slowly, so as not to spoil the quiff – and put his hand on the hatch. "And ..." I yelled. "*And* ... I've got a plastic scale model of Graceland."

His hand stopped at the hatch. "Oh, come on," he said. "You don't expect me to believe that?" There was a pause. "Do you?" he said. He wanted to believe it, I could hear he did.

There was a yammering howl all round us, like the whole Zoo had broken out at once. But I knew what it was. Security had been cock-a-hoop for weeks, with the news of their new snapper-dogs, the latest from the Genetics Control labs. The amplified voicebox, pitbull with a touch of Howler monkey, was just one of the features on the latest model.

Duckhead jumped for his cab. He wasn't any better friends with Security than me. The truck crunched into gear and I grabbed for the hatch, just as the first robo-doberman crashed against it. "Ivo," I yelled. "Help me close this thing." Too late, the dog had whirled round again – nothing stuns these creatures – and leapt again. This time its laser-tracked eyes got it right and it came straight through. That would have been it, I reckon, but the second and third of the things came after – pack coordination isn't perfect on this model – and knocked the first backwards, so they slithered on the garbage and the slashing teeth had missed me by an inch. I got my head to the opening; so did Ivo, and we jammed there, side by side.

"Duckhead!" I screamed. "Duckhead, mince!"

It may be that he heard me. I'd like to think so; I'm that sentimental. But I can imagine the calculations that might have clicked through his brain. Charge of aiding and abetting escape... Rich kid, must be something funny... Scip, up to something no good ... Whatever, Duckhead rammed the crusher screw in gear. Maybe he thought that by the time Security prised up the hatch they'd be peering into a well-compacted mess that might or might not have contained bits of me and Ivo. Whatever, he rammed it in gear.

What with the stink and the darkness and the slithery mess, the dogs hadn't quite found their footing. A moment more and they'd have been chewing us up from the heels. But the grinder coughed and there was a horrible sucking, everything gobbling backwards like slobbery lips and iron teeth. The howls of the dogs went from rage to panic, then a metal-grinding screech of pain.

4.

"You bilge-pig, Duckhead," I was spluttering as he hauled me out. "Why didn't you turn off the screw?"

Under the flat girdered roof of the service bunker the floodlight was dazzling. Twenty long-haul trucks, all slick chrome steel, stood glinting in it. Through the window of the comfort shack behind it, I could see the drivers munching through their textured protein packs, their eyes fixed on a screen on the wall. We were OK. The trucking station was miles out, where the one road cut into the hills. All round and beyond this was bare chalk and flinty rubble, where parched soil had blown away as dust. Beyond that, maybe, there would be the city; in between was this desert no one crossed unless they were desperate or were topdog types with leisure and a load of cred. We were OK. Surveillance didn't concern itself with life out here.

"It touched me..." Ivo shuddered weakly. "Another half an inch and..."

"Had to make sure, didn't I?" Duckhead gave a grin that could have been sly or it could have been foolish. With Duckhead you never can tell.

Through the door I saw drivers queuing at vend-o-mats. Everything was gleaming steel in there, even the stools and benches, made to last and bolted to the floor. Just then a huge man loomed through the doorway. At first I thought he was in chain mail, then I saw that the studs that bristled from his chest were implants in the skin. His enormous hand came up to brush us out of his way.

"Yo, Cuthbert," said Duckhead and they slapped palms, matey.

"What's these geeks?" grunted Cuthbert.

"Business, is all," Duckhead winked. Cuthbert nodded and lurched on.

"Just as well you got me with you," Duckhead murmured. "One word from *you...*" He was looking at Ivo. "Blokes like Cuth'd swat you like a fly." Ivo grinned uneasily. I didn't. They're no joke, these truckers. Loners, misfits – these are the basic qualifications for the job. To be an utter psycho seems to help. Apart from the casual roadkill, though, they don't get much chance to express it, in their cabs, alone.

"Touched me..." whimpered Ivo, head down on the steel bench. Duckhead clanked a litre mug of hyper-caff beside him.

"Get that down you," he said. "Then we talk terms." He glanced sideways at me. "If I was to find that you'd been lying about Graceland..."

"This kid," I said, passing over that, trusting to his

short attention span. "This kid is hot, hot property."

"Who is he, then?" Duckhead squinted. Ivo had his face in the mug of hypercaff, draining it. That stuff's meant to keep truckers awake through their twenty-hour shifts. What it would do to Ivo, I didn't like to think. But as he looked up a dull gleam lit up Duckhead's face. "Hey, hot jeeperooney," he breathed. "Ivo Maccaby!" He whooped and slapped his thigh. "Just in time. . ." He pointed to the big screen that held the truckers gawping at the wall. It was poor resolution, hardly any 3-D, almost last-millennium stuff, but you couldn't deny it was big. "Just in time for his own show!"

"Dreamtime Sleepcaps," purred the advert, as a slinky woman stretched and wriggled, a chrome dome covering most of her head so that only her blissed-out smile showed. "Night after night, you get the dreams you choose . . . with Dreamtime." Then – no credits, no titles, why bother when everyone knows – there was Ivo in action.

And action it was. He was running. An adventure sequence. Running, ducking through the shadows. The ambient track had thudding heartbeats, some-thing panting close behind him, sounds of pursuit, sounds of fear.

"Grrrreat," Duckhead chuckled. "I love chases." He might have noticed: I didn't agree.

There was a lull. The ten-foot-high screen-Ivo lay

still, and the music went all glissando, as he gazed out at the Creek.

"See," said Duckhead to me. "There are deep bits too. . ."

But Ivo, the real Ivo, was up on his feet. "No!" he yelled and hurled his mug at the screen. A shard or two of plastic clattered to the floor. A dozen truckers turned, not happy.

"They've got everything," wailed Ivo. "Everything! I don't know how, but they're bugging me now." As he raised his head to howl my eyes fell on the "I" shape at his throat.

"Ivo?" I said. "How long have you had that implant?"

He blinked, sniffing slightly. "Years," he said. "Long as I can remember. Dr Spellman said. . ." He trailed off. "What do you mean?" His hand came up to touch it. Then it struck him. "No!" he yelled again and started scratching at the implant. He grabbed a shard of plastic from the floor and started hacking at it. He winced and blood came, but it didn't shift.

"Don't!" I yelled. "God knows how it's wired up inside."

But he was stumbling to the door now. "Bugged!" he cried. "They bugged my body. I thought I could run away. But all this time they've been . . . *inside*!"

I guess we could have reasoned with him, but what could we say? *Go back, be happy, give them what they want?* As if he'd heard the thought in my head, he looked at me. "They're not going to have me," he said quietly. "I'm going to see to it." And he bolted through the door.

I guess we could have chased him and wrestled him down, but what then? As the door slammed I saw his pale shape flit across the forecourt, straight into the path of a truck. Fresh full of hypercaff, the driver saw him and reacted fast, swerving to a halt. The cab door opened and Cuthbert vaulted out. Ivo saw him. He could still have run but instead he stepped towards him, dancing slightly like a boxer, taunting him. Cuthbert stopped a moment, baffled. Ivo kicked him in the shin. Cuthbert's fist, with its mailed-knuckle implants, slammed out, one blow aimed straight at the head. And that was that.

I guess we could have stopped him, but what would that have achieved? Only to rob him of the only thing he could call his own: his choice. He said he'd make sure that they didn't have him, and that's what he did. He found how to be real. That's what I said to Duckhead, anyhow, as I climbed into his cab. The disposal men had moved in pretty quickly. They'd asked Duckhead if they could sling the body in the back with the rest of his rubbish, but even Duckhead couldn't face that.

"Poor brat," I said. I felt a kind of prickling, right back of my eyes, like I hadn't felt before. Duckhead clapped an arm around me. "Easy, kid," he said. "You want a story, I'll tell you a story. This one's about me..."

Governor: *Duckhead's Story*

1.

Whaaaay-ell, I thought to myself, *what have we here? Who's this little lady coming round the corner, straight into my patch? Hold it right there, lady, this is Duck-head's playspace.* "Hey, boss," Mundo muttered at my shoulder. "Can I off her now?" Always was crude, was Mundo. Me, I'm more curious. Right then, I wanted to know: this stranger in the purple jumpsuit, standing out a mile in the grey and mould-green of the precinct, just who does she think she is?

(You want to know? You bet you do. No one hitches a ride on Duckhead's truck without they listen to his story. They want to know, OK. I make that clear.)

Anyways... The gang clicked up the volume on their music blasters, first one then another, then another – different tracks of ancient Elvis blasting out of broken windows, or the same track ten times over, slightly out of sync. Tomcats mark their patch by scent; for us it was music. Two blocks over you ran into Korean techno-chanting: it was Dead Hand Clan land. That's how we knew who was who in the city. What was left of it, rather. They still had flood defences round it when I was a baby, but the tide kept rising. By the time I was out on the streets, there were just these islands in the waters of the scum lagoon.

"Hey, boys," this little lady hollered. Let her wait. She couldn't see where we were holed up, but she could hear. We sounded like a whole horde. Tell the truth, we had twice as many blasters as kids in the gang, since last year's mini-plague, but who was to know? I once saw a clip from this prehistoric 2-D film where one man defended a fort against hundreds, propping his dead mates up on the battlements and running from one to another now and then to fire their guns. It was getting a bit like that round our way. Yeah, you learn a lot from history.

"Hey, boys. Listen to me. Name's Niagra. I'm your friend." She was crazy. I respected that. There was a dull smash and a little lick of flame went up, ten paces in front of her. Just one of the little kids trying out a playschool Molly-cocktail, but it stopped her anyway. She looked up and round. "Duckhead? Dag? Mundo? Come on out. Let's do words."

I slipped out behind her, under cover of the music, so close I could see her startle when I spoke. Her breathing quickened but she steadied. Cool, that one. She turned and held her hands out in the safe-passage greeting. Were her fingers trembling, just a little? Whaay-ell, they'd better be.

"Duckhead!" she said. "Remember me?"

"Sorry, lady," I said very slowly. "Can't pretend I do."

"Neighbourhood Care Team. I covered this patch in the mini-plague. Got your girl Fleebie into sick bay just in time."

So that was it. Social worker! One moment the government was trying to wipe us off the streets, the next they were trying to make us *social*. Why couldn't they just leave us be? "Yeah," I said. "And into a police cell two days later. I remember that. We haven't seen her since. One of our best fighters, she was, Fleebie."

"Sorry. That was the N-Force order squad, not me."

I took a slow step forward. She didn't give ground, I grant her that. She stood there, jumpsuit flapping in the wind and the last licks of flame behind her. Now, I knew, and she knew I knew, that no Neighbourhood Care creep would ever set foot in our patch if there wasn't an armoured bus full of Neutralization Force heavies, the N-Forcers, not far out of sight. We could have offed her, easy – all it takes is a slingshot – but they'd have been round the corner before I could even turn to run. They were that caring, with Neighbour-hood Care.

Still, she was a cool one, you had to give her that.

"I've got an offer to make you," she said. "Free." Her smile let slip a flash of orthodonted middle classer's teeth. "New invention," she said. "It could do you some good."

"Let me guess. . ." I was pacing round her, back and forth and to and fro, putting the squeeze on her. "City's going to erect an Elvis theme park right here in our mall. New Graceland. And they're going to make me Major-Domo." I treated her to a glimpse of grey street-teeth.

Her grin shut off quick as a switch. "No joke. I mean, look at yourself. What are you doing?"

"Nothing. I'm not doing *nothing* . . . yet."

"You're pacing," she said. "Like a cat on splinters. Pacing."

"So?"

"That's stress. Tension. You're on edge. Nerves fraying. Every now and then they snap." My fist was bunching, but I wasn't going to give her the pleasure of saying: "told you so". "When," she went on, "did you last just relax?"

"I knew someone who did that once. Just once. The Dead Hand got him. RIP."

"Paranoia," she said. "It goes with tension. Over-reacting, lashing out, picking fights. Starting gang-fights when there's no real reason to."

I shrugged.

"It doesn't have to be that way," she said softly. "Have you ever thought: if you could keep con-trol. . .? Not go over the top? What kind of leader you could be then? Not just a little boss-cat – a real governor."

Mundo and Dag had ghosted out of cover right behind her. Behind them, the blank wall and the empty windows of Heartbreak Hotel, nerve-centre of the Duckhead empire. It was right at the edge now, one end on dry land, one in the water, and another few metres must have crumbled off at high tide last night. The slogan on the thirteenth floor read DONT STEP ON MY BLU SWAYD SH. . .

She sensed Mundo and Dag but she didn't turn round. "If I get any colder I'll have to ask your friends to toss another firebomb just to warm my trousers. Let's get inside and talk." Mundo had started tapping one palm with the crowbar in the other, regular, like keeping time. I knew what he'd be thinking: *Too much talk already*. But who was topdog in this precinct: Mundo, Dag, or me?

"We'll go to the penthouse," I said. "I need to interview this lady." Dag smiled thinly. She'd be thinking: *time for fun and games*. Dag always had a soft spot for a bit of casual torture. But upstairs on the landing I said, "Wait outside, you two." They looked at each other. "Anything you say, boss." That's when I knew for certain: I was going to have a problem here.

"Look at the state of it," Niagra was saying. Imagine that. There she was in Heartbreak Hotel, with Duckhead, governor of all this, and she looked around and said it just like that. Kids had gone out of that window for less. "I mean *look* at it."

It was one of those pollution evenings, purplish like a bruise. The light caught the splinters round the window's edge, rather beautiful, I thought. There was more light on the lagoon than in the sky and out of habit I scanned for shadows moving, an N-Force snatch squad or the Dead Hand horde out raiding from the next block. I used to watch from the penthouse, most nights, with the biggest blaster on to warn all comers: "*Feel so lonely, baby. Feel so lonely I could DIE...*" When the gang sang along with Elvis, of course, we sang "*you*," not "*I*".

"Do you like it?" said Niagra. "Living like this..."

"*Like* it?" Stupid question. Everyone who *liked* it, the folk from the cosy uphill suburbs, had left it while they still could. They knew the score, they heard the forecasts and they knew the polar ice was melting. They knew how little time the city had left. It seemed slow coming, but when it happened it was sudden. The topdoggers cut and ran; the authorities pulled the plug on food defences and the slums went under. That's when people like me came into our own. You could see where the islands would be, if you weren't stupid. You spotted natural fortresses, like this peninsula of ours, that would only take a line of barricades... Or command posts like the crumbling cliff-face of

Heartbreak Hotel. Sure, we made ourselves at home in no time. But *like* it? words like that didn't apply.

"You're too close together, that's the trouble," said Niagra. Out in broad daylight her skin had looked matt black but here in the evening light there was a purple sheen on it, especially her cheeks when she smiled. "We aren't built for it. Even in the old days it was trouble – road rage, murder at the traffic lights. . ." I wasn't really attending. I was thinking how Dag's face went all hard and pale out on the stairs, and how she moved alongside Mundo, how they looked at me. Making plans. Every gang governor used to be somebody else's trusted right-hand man.

"Adrenalin," Niagra said suddenly. "That's the enemy. Makes you sharp and edgy, like a speed-drug in the brain. Just when you should be thinking clear and cool, there's a shot of adrenalin. You grab for the knife or the slingshot, you can't help it. You're not in control."

Across the water someone had made someone a present of a firebomb. A cloud of smoke went up, with flame inside it; its reflection went down, fading, like it was sinking through the sludge of the lagoon.

"They've invented a gizmo," she went on. "Big public health campaign. Back in the petrol age they fitted lorries with a little box that stopped them going too fast. Saved fuel, saved lives. They called it a *governor*," she said. "That's why I thought of you."

"You want to save me petrol?"

"I mean," she said more slowly, "there's this little implant you can have, very tidy, in the back where the adrenal glands are. Keeps you really calm and cool. They're fitting them free."

"Hold on." I was getting the picture. "This is one of those experiments."

"That's where you're wrong," she said, serious. "It's the latest thing. Levelling out, they call it. They're all doing it, out in the timeshares. '*You on the level?*' they say to each other." My eyes were straying to the window, thinking of the splash she'd make. "No, listen," she said quickly. "Topdoggers like that, they know what's good for them." The mushroom cloud out yonder seemed to have hit the smog ceiling and was picking up the sunset, simply hanging there. "How old are you? Sixteen?"

I shrugged. There are some things a man doesn't talk about.

"You'll be old by thirty. While your average middleclasser with a governor will reach, oh, a hundred and fifty, easy..."

"Hold on," I said. "Why should you ... why should the government want to make *us* live longer?"

"Just want to keep everyone happy," she said. "That's Neighbourhood Care for you."

Just then the curtain on the door ripped open. "We think," said Mundo, striding in, "that there's been too much talking."

Dag nodded. "We think," she said, glancing at Niagra, "that you're forgetting who's friend and who's foe round here." They had moved round behind her but it was me they were looking at. So this was it. One false move, it would be me going out of that window, and the ghetto-blasters would be playing Dag and Mundo's music. Time to exercise a bit of leadership.

"Hey," I said. "How's about a bit of entertainment?" I grabbed Niagra by the arm and jerked her to the window. "OK," I shouted, "you N-Force bastards out there, Duckhead's got your agent. Why doncha come on in and get her – if you dare?"

"Duckhead, you mashbrain," said Dag, but her eyes lit up. Never could resist a fight, could Dag. I was counting on it. Outside there was the thud of motors. Yeah, they'd been listening in, the N-Force, like I knew they would. My heart was revving, too. That was it, just like the little lady said: adrenalin. "The Big Machine," I said, on the spur of the moment. "Let's do it in style. Haven't had a real old-world joyride for years!"

"You're crazy," said Niagra. "You want a ransom? Do a deal now while there's time." Then, on second thoughts, she shrugged. "Nah, they wouldn't pay."

"Why not?"

"Because," Niagra said, "it's me. I've been fired from my last three jobs. *Questioning instructions,* that's what the charge-sheet said. What else do you think I'm doing working a rat-patch like this?"

There was a crump in the courtyard nine floors down – a percussion grenade. Half the blasters cut out at once; there was the crunch of running feet and the *whoosh* of some firebombs in answer.

"Out the window with her," said Mundo. "Let's get going." Downstairs there was a crump and a shriek as the N-Forcers reached the booby-trap zone on the second floor. It slowed them a moment, then they were thumping on up, sprinkling each new room with gunfire. The megaphone coughed: "*Come out with your hands up. Throw down your weapons. Send the hostage out alone.*"

Niagra was shaking her head. "Don't," she said. "I know them. They're bored and angry. They'll blast anyone who steps through that door. Me or you."

"I thought they were your friends," I said.

She laughed. "It's just a job."

Dag and Mundo were watching us, dead cold. "She stays with us," I said. "Any other questions? No? Then let's take a spin. Let's show those metalheads down there whose playspace this is. Let's go!"

The Emergency Exit. It was the quick way down, or the quickest bar one, the hundred-metre dive, which we saved for particular enemies. The balcony sloped out above the water, not that deep but sinister, blackish purple, with top-storey walls of buildings rotting in it like bad teeth. Near the edge, we'd lashed a pulley to a girder. For the first time that day Niagra went a little grey.

Then her N-Force buddies ripped through the floor beneath us and I could see her weighing it up: the lesser of two evils. The pulley screeled as Dag and Mundo went down. Up came the counterweight, scrap metal engine parts lashed to the end of the metal hawser like a bunch of clanking fruit. It shuddered at the top for a moment, then dropped again. Next, please...

Niagra's mouth opened as if she might have been about to argue. But things moved faster than that. There was a clatter on the stairs, a garbling megaphone voice and then the shock-wave of a stun-grenade. We were lucky we were balanced on the edge; it just kicked us off cleanly. I grabbed at the rope and somehow Niagra made it too. Good reactions. Not for the first time I thought: *never underestimate that lady*. Not the first time, nor the last.

The pulley screeched and we were swinging wide above the water. Just a blur of shredded balconies, quick as a cardsharp's shuffle, then thump: we shuddered to a stop, a metre from the water, then we swung in, hauling out like beached fishes on to concrete which, for all it was slimy and cold, felt like home.

Upstairs everything was quiet. The N-Force would

be glaring through their visors with their bloodlust up, orders burned on their brains and no one there to neutralize. With luck they'd shoot each other up in sheer frustration. It's been known.

"Let's move," snarled Mundo. Dag had Niagra by the arm, twisting it back in a mean lock. "Don't even think of running, sugar. Don't know where we're going, but you're coming too."

2.

Down the slope to the underground car park there was darkness as thick as a wall. It should have been flooded but the water hadn't broken through yet; you thought of that every time you went there. It gave it a special feeling. I guess you'd call it awe. You see, this was the sanctum, the Holy of Holies. Even then, we didn't just barge in, even with the N-Force squad pounding at our heels. That's the trouble with people today – they got no *reverence*. So we paused. There was that special hush around us and, like nothing else on earth, that smell!

The past, that's what it was. Makes me weep now to think of it. The old world! Incense of ancient exhaust fumes, of sump oil and that special touch of diesel. Mundo struck a flint; a taper flared; our shadows flickered, black stains on the concrete walls. And there, as our eyes adjusted, we saw it, in the furthest corner – just an outline, like a creature crouching. Then the torchlight struck its ancient chrome. Four round eyes, and a radiator grille liked bared teeth, panting. Yes, it was the Cadillac. The Big Machine.

We weren't the first to worship it, I knew that. Somebody in the suburbs had rescued it from way beyond this century; he'd cleaned it and cared for it and oiled and waxed it till it gleamed. He'd made his pile in the motor trade when there was one; when all the other topdog types were scuttling off to timeshares for a long, long holiday, this one stayed in the city, in a private theme park of his own. He was ancient himself when the flood came. By the time the kids had scaled the outer walls, with the laser wire and all, they weren't feeling friendly. They'd trashed five or six other antique motors before I even reached the scene. They had the old guy lashed to the bonnet of the Cadillac and they were going to torch the two of them together, but I said, "No. Don't touch it or you die." It seemed the least I could do. I mean, he was going to snuff it naturally, but the limousine... I think that gave him some small pleasure as they dragged him away.

The first true relic I ever laid hands on was a poster so faded you could see the light right through it: Elvis leaning, kind of casual, on what could have been the exact same model. Yellow, wide as a street, with fins at the back like it was thinking about growing wings. The King could have cruised in it; now it was ours. The last car, I mean *real* car, in the sinking city, maybe in the world, who knows?

But I'm getting carried away. You do when you're feeling religious. But Mundo and Dag were impatient.

They had never really got the point about the Big Machine. They treated it like it's just, well, a *machine*. That was their problem: no soul. I pushed past them and patted the fender and it seemed to quiver.

Tonight's the night, old beast, I thought. *You're going to roar again.*

"Hold tight." We came up that ramp so fast you'd have thought we were going to fly. There was a posse of N-Forcers lined up in their battle-gear but they were still looking up at the building, and before they'd figured what the noise was we'd smashed through the cordon, sending armoured tandems spinning, riders thrown aside like litter in the wind. I slowed at the corner, just long enough to let them gather their wits. What's the point of a joyride if they're don't even see which way you went? Where's the buzz in that? Besides, if the cops wouldn't play, what would I do with Dag and Mundo? They were so charged up now that one way or another sparks had got to fly.

The armoured tandems slewed round, motors whining. Then I was revving so hard the Big Machine seemed to stand up and paw at the air. The tyres bit and we were off like a rat down a gutter. These were our backstreets, we knew every inch. This was our kingdom, our small corner of this mouldy drowning city. It was our element, and tonight was the night.

Night vision. That was our secret weapon. We knew every rut and we knew where the pavements had buckled and where cracks had opened into drowned basements below. We knew where an alley would drop without warning into some slimy back reach of lagoon. I sliced round the back of the precinct and the air drummed with the glorious thunder of internal combustion as I opened up the throttle full.

"Hell," Niagra yelled, impressed. "What *is* this thing? What does it run on?" Not every neighbourhood still had petrol. Most of the little that had been left in filling station forecourts had been used for firebombs in the early skirmishes. In my patch, we'd eked it out carefully. We were conservationists. By all the standards that mattered thereabouts, we were rich.

What I didn't say, because even Mundo didn't know yet, was that this tankful was the last. This was the Big Machine's last outing, ever. That was why this had to be the joyride to end all joyrides. We were going to make it *good*.

The lights of the armoured bikes showed behind us as I screeched out into Memphis Boulevard. I leaned back, one hand on the wheel with its pink fun-fur wheel-cosy and glanced at Niagra. She was pinned in the back, part by the G-force of acceleration, part by Dag's elbow in her throat. "We're cruisin'. . ." I yelled, trying to sound casual like Elvis. "Relax. Enjoy."

We made a noise, you bet we did. At all the empty-looking windows, the ruined doorways, faces appeared. There'd be kids from our horde and there'd be loners. The city was full of them, outcasts, misfits of all kinds hoping to claw their way back to the dry-land suburbs, though we all knew no one made it nowadays. They came crawling out of their holes now, as if it was a party. It was the least I could do, as governor of this patch: lay on a good show. There'd be wandering tribes and grim little family groups, all weasel-eyed, watching each other's backs, expecting to be mugged at any moment, but still they'd run to the window, gape and clap and cheer.

The lights swung out of the alley behind us. Not one of those bikes could take an old combustion engine in a straight race. Then my pulse changed gear. Another line of lights moved out to block the way in front.

I slammed into a skid-turn. Dag yelped, but I knew my way round. As the lights closed in, I gunned towards a wall – a wooden gate – ripped through it in a cloud of splinters, sent an industrial-sized dustbin flying and slewed to a halt in the yard. A tribe of kids scattered like mice. I was out of the driving seat in one leap. Mundo was alongside, and three or four kids from the yard; together we trundled the bin to the gate and gave it a heave-ho out into the boulevard. It got there in time for the bikes. They were slowing, wondering where we'd got to, but still travelling at speed. The pillion-gunmen loosed a round of fire at the thing that was trundling at them, then there was a trail of sparks and the first bike cartwheeled and another and another, caught it head on.

I was back in the driving seat, foot down. We roared out of the gate and slammed back the way we'd come.

In the rear-view I could see the lights of the N-Force bikes getting back in formation. In the back seat Niagra was struggling to look. And there was a new sound. Over the roar of the car a steady beat had started, clash-clash-clash, like something chewing metal. They were out on the pavements in hundreds, more people than I knew our block had in it, and they were banging dustbin lids, old hubcaps, anything that made a din. They were crowding the edge of the road, almost into our path. I saw faces cheering, mouths wide open, as they flickered past. What were they doing, coming out of cover now of all times, asking for it, jeering at the N-Force bikers as they put their foot down for the race? It was stupid and wonderful and I noticed that my mouth was open, *wha-a-a-y-eee!* cheering these crazy no-hope people, my people, citizens of Duckhead's kingdom. Then there was a crackling of fire behind us as the pillion-gunmen raked the crowd.

They were scattering now; some falling, some running. Some regrouped in doorways, hurling bricks and bars and stones. The N-Forcers' headlights flailed about a moment, then they were settling in a tight defensive ring. The sparks of their gun-blasts jabbed out like a crown of thorns. I slammed through a full turn on the handbrake, then took aim, Duckhead to the rescue, my foot on the gas and my hand on the horn.

The crowd broke just in time, or most of them. The N-Forcers were slower. Some might have jumped free of their bikes but I couldn't tell because I'd ducked beneath the dashboard – oh, the lovely wood-look plastic dashboard – just before we hit. For a moment it was thunder and lightning; I was slammed up hard against the steering column, then we were screeching sideways and I couldn't tell which way was up or down.

When we spun to a stop I got my head up, but there was nothing much to see. The crowd had closed in over the N-Forcers like the lagoon closes over a dumped body. There was no gunfire and no head-lights, so I guessed they'd need no help from me. Beneath the buckled yellow bonnet of the Cadillac there was a sickly wheeze of steam.

A groan from the back seat. "Well?" I said, though my voice came out a bit high and wobbly. "Do we have a problem back there?"

"I think your friend's in shock," said Niagra. "And she's leaning on my face. What now?"

The heli-gunship came down the boulevard quite slowly, thudding, not much higher than the buildings.

There were searchlight beams beneath it, panning to and fro as if it was walking on two legs. As one reached the crowd a jet of skunk-gas blossomed and the crowd went stumbling and choking but the two beams went on pacing, sort of ghostly, through the falling mist.

I fired the stalled engine once, twice. It gave another sick wheeze. On the third time it chugged into action, missing beats and struggling as we backed through what might have been a plate glass window in the age of shopping, long ago.

The searchlight beam just clipped our bumper. It was so buckled they must have thought we were the kind of wreckage they expect to find round here. The gunship slipped off sideways, out of sight. "They're gone," said Mundo. But not far. The sound of rotors settled to an anxious throb.

"You didn't think they'd just go home," said Niagra. "Carefully controlled revenge – one of the principles of Neutralization Force theory."

"Carefully controlled?"

"Yeah, well, that's the theory," she said. "Me, I'd scatter now. You got a secret bunker?" Just at that moment the sound of rotors rose and swung off fast, out across the lagoon. There was a deep dull *crrrrump* and a new light in the sky, bluish white for a moment then gradually reddening and turning to a steady flicker. I could guess already where they'd been.

By the time we reached the Precinct I could make out the bare bones of Heartbreak Hotel, outlined by flames. It was like a whole creature, alligator or a mega-rat perhaps, being barbecued. Then floor by floor it all started folding inwards, breaking up in the heart of the fire.

The gunship idled for a minute, out over the lagoon. Then it seemed to shrug – job done – and cut off home, wherever home might be. There was no music in the precinct – all my carefully-hoarded digi-tabs of Elvis would be crisping, melting. There was no sound but the gentle crunch and hiss of flames.

"Is that it?" Dag said. "End of the show? The bastards!"

She was pacing now, thumping a fist in the palm of her hand. "Let's get back to the boulevard," she said. "Maybe they've left us an N-Forcer we can play with. No..." She swung round, knife in hand. She was looking at Niagra. "No, we've got one here."

"Ah, leave it. I'm tired." The bright light had gone out; everything had gone monochrome. I could feel the anticlimax setting in.

"I've not finished," said Dag.

"Someone mention a ransom?" Mundo muttered, as if he'd dozed off for the last hour and come to again.

"I want to stop this lady staring at me," Dag said. "I don't like her eyes." She gave her special smile. "Let's have fun."

"I don't feel like it, OK?" I said, as sharp as I could, but everything felt heavy. As suddenly as a car can run out of petrol, you can run dry of adrenalin. Out over the bay the islands looked like burnt-out bonfires, piles of blackened sticks with just an ember glowing here and there. Heartbreak Hotel was smouldering. Everything felt cold. "Hell, what's the point?" I said.

Dag swung round at me. "Point? What's the *point* of anything, mashbrain? What's the point of all *this*?" She was staring out over the islands, throwing her arm out like she'd tossed a firebomb. "What's the point of someone like *her* telling us to be *happy* in the middle of all this? What's the point of Duckhead, our governor, our hardman, going soft and listening to her? None of this would have happened if we'd offed her like I said we should."

"Watch it." I was on my feet now. "Where'd you be without me? Rats in a hole. Cause I'm the only one round here who's got *imagination*. Take tonight. It was a great show."

"Great?" spat Dag, squinting into the flames.

"And the motor..." said Mundo, like his dog's died.

"And the petrol," Dag said. "Blown it. Blown it all. And why?"

"It was a great show. The last joyride, and the best. We'll live for ever. We're a legend now."

"Words!" Dag snarled. "I'm going to out somebody

in a minute." Suddenly Niagra – she'd been quiet for the last bit – spoke.

"You see?" she said. "Adrenalin. . ."

"Shut up, you," I said. "It was great this evening, great . . ." But I couldn't go on. "Look at us. There's nowhere else . . . there's no *way* else for us to be."

"There could be," she said. "I could show you."

I caught the flash of Dag's knife as she jumped at Niagra and I lashed out at her arm, not accurate but quick enough just to turn it away. The knife spun out across the precinct. My knife was out now as well, a matter of instinct, and I was hefting it in Mundo's direction too. He tried to hold my gaze a moment but he was weary, I could see it. Two hours ago, they'd been planning a coup. There was not much left to off the boss for now. Mundo looked at the ground.

"Me and Niagra here, we're doing words, OK?" I shouted after Dag and Mundo as they backed away. "Words, you know? You should try them sometime."

3.

Strange to think, from out here on the Beach, that there's still a city somewhere. Or I guess there must be, or where do all these timeshare people come from? It can't have all gone under, though it's years since I saw it. One thing's for sure, the land that's left, it won't be for the likes of you and me.

But picture it that night, as me and Niagra pushed the boat out on the dark lagoon. The islands, silhouettes of islands, ragged round the edges with the buildings flooded but not yet gone under. Even out in the deeps there were top floors of buildings way down, maybe twenty storeys high. They would look quite solid, and expensive like penthouses used to be, but way down below the foundations were weakening. Some mornings you'd look out and, what d'you know, another would be gone.

The city... It was like an alligator in the shallows, nose and eyes and tail-tip showing, can't tell if it's dead or sleeping or about to lash out, clamp you in its jaws and drag you down. Strange to think what was there once, houses and shops, fresh running water, streetlights and, oh, cars, cars, cars. I still get dreams: parades of them, all shapes and sizes, family saloons, trucks, racers, soft tops, station waggons, lining every boulevard and alley, filling the air with their throbbing warm breath, as fabulous as dragons. All before my time, of course, though when I was small I heard the oldies talking, and I've seen old 2-D film clips. Or maybe I just breathed it in without knowing, some nights when I went down on my own to sit in silence with the Big Machine.

Oh hell, it makes my eyes go blurry, thinking of the Big Machine.

Anyway, me and Niagra...There was just enough moon in the clouds for me to see the little slipway as we nudged the boat in. It was quite a big island, or part of the mainland maybe, though I'd have expected surveillance if so. But Niagra knew where we were going. Once we were on dry land, she went first and I followed, close.

Let's be clear about this: she was my hostage. I'd got a gun in my shirt and she hadn't, as simple as that. Quite what use a hostage was when no one was coming after her, when in fact they were glad to be rid of her, I couldn't be sure. I had a feeling they wouldn't have taken her back if I'd delivered her to security headquarters wrapped in paper and pretty pink bows.

Up ahead the perimeter fence looked ugly, with touch-sensitive razor twine on top, the kind that would lash round and slice you into noodles, one move out of place. But she made for the foot of the fence; there was a turnstile. That was all, just a door made of steel spikes on a spindle in a steel-barred frame. I gave it a push; it turned one way, easy. "Stop!" Niagra clamped my wrist. "Don't do a thing I don't tell you," she whispered. "Not a thing, or we're meat."

I'll give it to them, some of these auto-security firms: they come up with the goods. There was a second turnstile just inside the first one, so close that the spikes overlapped. That was where you found the palm-pad and the voiceprint grille. If your palm print and voice fitted, then you just walked through. If not, the turnstiles gave a spin. Minced and blended. As Niagra said, you were meat.

"Thing is," she said, very low, "if they've cancelled my access..."

"How will you know?" She just looked at the steel spikes and stroked her hand along one, like a sleeping dog with a terrible bite.

"The other thing is," she went on, "we only get one go. Both of us go through together. It'll be a squeeze."

Another time, another place, the next bit might have been a pleasure, squirming in so close against her that her tight curls scratched my cheek. I felt her breathing, quick and shallow; I couldn't be sure if that heartbeat was hers or mine. We were inside the blender. She reached out a palm and laid it on the pad.

Nothing happened. She was trembling. Then she took a deep breath and said "Niagra K. Birmingham: N-Care agent 896B" clear and loud.

There was a pause, then a small buzz in the turnstile's workings. Don't breathe. Then: click, and the second gate released.

"Wheeee-oo," she said quietly, and sank down on the grass. So she can't have been "on the level". I thought back to the things I'd seen her do that day. She had no governor keeping her steady; she done all that for herself. Yeah, that was some lady, even if she was a social worker. That's true cool for you.

But the place ... I couldn't figure it. We seemed to have stepped into a movie from another century. A wide and quiet street. So much space it was scary. I mean, where did you dive for cover when the snipers started? On either side were houses, small and square and separate, with a patch of grass in front of each. They'd got glass in the windows, whole panes, not one broken, so they glinted in soft orange street light. There were little boxes on the sills with plants in. Some of the grass squares had a round pond with a small guy fishing. Otherwise they were the same.

"What *is* this?" I said again. "Some kind of theme park? A rich kids' style camp?" But there was a sad feeling, not all sad but like a smell you can't place, sort of sweet and musty, rising up inside me, like a memory from way back, though it couldn't be. I'd never seen anything like this in my life. It must be the strain of the day. "No," she said. "This is NeuTown. People live here. Really. People like you." I must have laughed out loud, because she laid her hand on my arm and looked me in the eye. "I know what you're thinking: where's the street patrols, where's the barricades and sentries? They don't need them. Everybody's on the level here."

Now it had to be a dream, because we were walking down the middle of the road, right in the open, and no one had plugged us with a slingshot, no one'd laid us out in the gutter to rifle our pockets or stuck a knife in our ribs just casually to see how sharp it was. In short, it wasn't natural. But I was following Niagra. What else could I do?

"Here," she said. "Let's try this one. There are people you might like to meet."

It took two or three rings on the doorbell before a light came on behind the glass door. A man's shape appeared inside, stumbling a little as if we'd woken him. Not a guard or lookout, but a man in striped pyjamas, looking like he'd got up from a pleasant sleep.

"What a nice surprise," he said mildly. He was holding the door open, fancy that, wide open so it framed him like a target in a shooting gallery. "Niagra. And . . . do I know your friend here? Come on in."

"Take a pew," he said, leading us into a room that

was all soft, with soft stuff on the floor and bulgy seats to sit on. As he flicked the light on I blinked: everything, even the walls, was flower patterns, all soft pinks and greens and blues. "Try the new sofa," he smiled. "I know what you need: a nice cup of tea."

I stared at his back as he padded to the kitchen. I'd heard of New Normal, quite a fashion thing a few years back, but you could see that beneath the short-back-and-sides, shirts and ties those kids were keeping a hand on their flick knives. They never sported dressing-gowns and carpet slippers.

"Niagra!" Odd, I felt I'd got to whisper, so he wouldn't hear. "Tell me this is some weird Virtual. Please..."

She grinned. "Sorry, all this must be quite a shock for you. Lots of places used to be like NeuTown, more or less. The government's sunk quite a lot of cred to build it, and put people in it. Like Wilfred here, and..."

"That's another thing," I interrupted. "What's wrong with this guy? He's so ... nice."

"He's on the level, of course," said Niagra. "And this is a Show Home, to show kids like you how different life could be..."

"Yeah? And why did he look at me like that, as if ... as if he knew me?"

"Because he does. He was the first one from your end of town to be fitted with a governor. Don't you recognize him?" Just then the guy walked back through the door and I stared. Stare like this in the street and the other guy either runs or he squares up and outs you. Not this one: he simply smiled at me.

"Oh god, Wildboy Cutler!" I gasped.

He grinned back as if it's a joke. Last time I'd seen him he had barbed-wire dreadlocks and an extra set of metal teeth. We'd been at knife-point with each other in a skirmish round the Back Reach. I'd thought then, if one of us didn't off the other we should team up, start a whole new horde. Then the N-Force moved in and we never had the conversation. Pity, could have changed a bit of history.

"I prefer Wilfred these days," he said in that soft voice. "Here, get this tea inside you. Wait a minute, I'll call Mary. She'd be disappointed not to have a chat with you."

There was a silence, a minute, after Wildboy – sorry, Wilfred – called upstairs. Then a gentle *pad-pad* coming down. Wilfred stood holding the door open, beaming, as if this was all his own work and he just *knew* that we'd like it. "Mary, dear," he said. "We've got guests. Miss Niagra and, I'm sorry, I forget your name."

The pair of them didn't bat an eyelid even when I started to scream. The girl adjusted her frilly nightie and patted her curly hair back as if it might be that that was bothering me. Well, it was part of it. Last time I'd seen her it was stripes of mauve and green, just to clash with her warpaint.

"Fleebie!" I cried. I mean *shouted*, but there were tears on my cheeks, I really was crying. "What have they done to you?"

"Duckhead! So you're on the level too? I'm so glad. You must come round and see the new patio. Wilfred's so good at garden design..."

There was a complicated double smash or three. I'd picked up the glass-topped coffee table and hurled it through the double-glazed window. Wilfred and Mary were gazing at the jagged hole, looking mildly puzzled, as I leapt through. Outside on the street I was running and not looking back, even when the sound of a siren started up and a squad car swung into the street. There were folk coming out of their houses, standing framed on porches, husbands with one arm around wives' shoulders, mildly muttering "Oh dear." Then somebody jumped from the shadows and grabbed me.

"Idiot!" Niagra whispered. "If you wanted to go, you could have just *said*..." She dragged me to my feet. "You've ruined it. You can't stay now..."

"But... That's not Fleebie really, is it?"

"Sure it is. She's happy."

"How could they?" I said. "How could they *do* that to her? Was it torture? Drugs? Or what?"

"Sorry, Duckhead," said Niagra, and her eyes went

large as if she was truly sorry. "I don't know how to say this, but . . . she volunteered."

I scarcely noticed as Niagra slid us through the automatic turnstile. Outside, I sank to my knees. Across the dark water the islands of the sinking city were waiting, one with Duckhead's patch, his style, his music printed all over it. Or it had been, until today.

It was a great live show, that final car chase. No one would ever forget it on the island. Duckhead and his Big Machine! We'd be a legend. How we took on the N-Force squad and won. Guess that made me a hero, till the sun came up and they got to count how many of our own horde ended up dead.

And Mundo and Dag. . . It would be their music in the blasters, no more Elvis, no more style.

"Home, then?" said Niagra. I didn't know what she was doing here, why she'd brought me here at all. Yes, I knew it was her job, the social worker business, but she'd blown that when she stepped into Heart-break Hotel. It was almost – though this is ridiculous – almost as though she cared. As though she'd taken all these risks for me.

"Home?" I said. "Where's that?"

Niagra squinted at me. "You'd better sort that for yourself. I'm off."

"What?" I said, then: "Hey, hold it, you're forgetting. You're my hostage. I'm still governor round here."

With a swift move she ducked under my guard, one foot whipped up and smacked me in the vitals. As I doubled up she clamped my arm. It smacked on the ground and the gun went spinning to the water's edge. She kicked it over.

"Sorry," she said, and really sounded like she meant it. She swayed on her feet, in calm martial-arts balance, waiting to see if I'd try anything. No way. She smiled down, not unkindly.

Now I saw: she could have done that any time she wanted. That was what hurt. She could have gone back to Neighbourhood Care, picked up another job in another dumb precinct, peddling peace and calm to kids who don't know what it means. Here was a lady who could do anything she wanted, I thought, and who could stop her? She could have escaped, no sweat. It made me feel sort of insulted. And yet. . .

"If I were you," she said, "I'd head round the wire, then uphill to the depot. It's a trucking station, shipping garbage to and from the timeshares. Dirty work and you get attacked by trashtypes all the time. On the other hand, no one asks questions." She shrugged. "It's a life, at least."

"So what's the alternative?" I said, and we both laughed. Kind of rueful, it was, but it was the first time we'd both laughed together all that long, long day.

Sand Golem

It was half a day's walk down from the trucking station. I kept to the gullies, deep scars down the hillside left by flash floods like some big cat had been sharpening its claws. I figured that way there'd be shade but as the sun got high it vanished. Frilled stone-coloured lizards watched me, front right leg and back left lifted, panting. By the time I reached the outskirts I'd squeezed out the water pack Duck-head had given me; soon I'd be stumbling. I'd never been so glad to see the rat-heaps of the Outer Lots before.

They weren't waiting for me but they saw me coming. Sprawled in the shade of a tipped concrete slab they were, twenty or so trashtypes, while the sun beat like a hammer on the dust outside.

They were doing what you did when it was too hot to stir there at Psylicon Beach – just staring. You could watch the timeshares warp and shiver in the heat haze. You could watch the armoured transport trucks, one an hour, crawl up the hill and over, solar cells extended (if there's too much sun, why waste it?) like grey butterflies kitted out for battle. You could dream, if you were a trashtype, dreams of where they were headed, to the city, where cred flowed like water and the things you'd heard about came true.

"Hey ... Scip! Talk of the devil. . ."

Maddog's voice, out of the shadow. Damn. I raised a hand in greeting and walked on. In a bound he was out there in front of me.

"Sorry," I said. "Can't stop. Got business. . ."

"You got business here, friend." Under the brim of his cap a few odd teeth flashed a Maddog grin. "We really, *really* want a word with you."

With a bound he was up to me, snatching my hat. The sun's heat hit my bare head like an iron bar. Maddog backed beneath the concrete, sniggering. "Come into the shade. We've saved a place for you."

"OK," I said, as if I had some option. It can boil your brains, five minutes flat, this kind of weather. "Since you ask so nicely, maybe I will."

If you didn't know they were kids you'd think they were a rag pile blown there by the wind. That's what they find so quaint, upstreamers, when they come round with their cameras. They take movies of it to impress their friends back home. Out in the Outer Lots, you put whatever you can find between you and the sun, as much as you can of it, stitched up loose for coolness. It's the guests in the timeshares who can go round semi-naked, all cool, pale and fashionable. Even the black skintypes look cool and pale in there. Pale is a state of mind and money. It takes colonnades and fountains, sunblock windows and chilled air. In short, pale costs you cred. Out in the Lots, you make do with what you find.

"Scip," said Maddog. "We got a bone to pick with you."

Twenty trashtype faces peering from the shadow, all with that sandblasted look. A few of them had darker blotches, sun curse, that would spread and spread. We don't mention Ultra-Violet, we don't talk about cancer. If we did, we'd be talking about it all the time.

Guppy was there, too, wild kid from the servants' quarters. She gets everywhere, does Guppy, maybe because the guards at the gate think she's cute, if they don't lift their visors and investigate. Maybe she's so small she slips right through the wire. You'd think she'd get eaten alive out here, till you look in her eyes. You try to eat Guppy, she'd stick in your teeth.

"You told us a story," said Maddog slowly. "The one about the . . . the. . ." He glanced round at the others.

"The Ghoul," one put in.

"No, the Goalie," said another.

"The Golem?"

"Yeah, that one. Well, it *wasn't true!*"

There was a bad pause. Sometimes I trade with

them, fair deals like everything else. In exchange for information, the kind of stuff they notice sneaking round the wire, I give them some of what I've got. Stories. Not BeMovies, but the real kind, from the books I've got out in the Tower with my hoard of other old-world stuff. That's where I got the Golem story, all rotting leather on the outside and the words in gold print: *The Golem Of Prague*. Tales about monsters, misshapes, creatures that didn't quite turn out right – it's not hard to guess why they appeal to me.

"It's a story," I said. "Stories don't have to be true." But Maddog wasn't in a mood to argue.

"You said they made this giant, right? You said they made him out of mud. Right? Right! You said he was big and strong."

"Uh-huh." I knew they'd like that bit. In the story these long-ago people, the Jews, were being pushed around by all the topdogs of the time. They weren't so good at fighting, the Jews, though pretty good at stories, and one of them had this idea – to make a giant, just like Maddog said. There was something in the Golem story that had really got them: how the trashtypes of another time had struck back. If they could then, why not us now? It must have hit home with Maddog: he'd remembered, with his sandfly-sized attention span.

"Well..." said Maddog slowly. "It doesn't work."

"It's a *story*," I said again.

He crunched my hat with his fist. "Don't you play words with me. We made one, out there on the beach. We did the chanting, walked in circles, all that. And it didn't work. The thing just lay there."

I could have blown my chances then and laughed, but there was something in his eyes, real menace. And the others, too. No one was laughing, though Guppy had this kind of twinkle in her eyes. *This is new*, she'd be thinking to herself, *to see Scip in a fix. How's he going to get himself out of this one?* I was starting to wonder, myself.

"Hold on," I said. "It was probably just an early form of BeMovie, that's all..." Then I stopped. It's funny how danger can sharpen your thinking – the thought, for example, that if I didn't come up with the goods somehow, Maddog might just have me staked out in the sun to fry. But my mind went back to the Sherbet Fountain, how there'd been a team of BeTech consultants all over the place wiring up a new system, and the old gear... I happened to know, the way you pick up things when it pays you to listen, that some of the old gear had been slipped off to the Major-Domo's quarters, for his private entertainment. In the old days I wouldn't have known, but he was getting careless. Since the alligator trouble, rumour had it that the M-D had hit the Liquid Moon. Things were slipping at the Sherbet Fountain. What's more, he had this grudge against me, as if what had happened with the alligator hadn't been fair game.

"Hey," I said to Maddog. "Give me an hour, I'll see what I can do. . . ."

"You're not going nowhere," said Maddog. "You think I'm stupid?"

"How can I fix it if I'm stuck out here?"

He shrugged. Then Guppy piped up. There are things about that kid I'd never fathomed. "You want an errand run?" she said. "You'll owe me." I looked down at her, knee high to an alligator.

"OK," I said. "You got a deal."

"They got the stuff!" called Maddog. Guppy came over the dust towards us, grinning. An hour flat, she'd done it. Eight or ten trashtypes were dragging through the dust behind her, hauling tarnished boxes, loose wires, battered power cells. It looked as if one half of a scrap heap had picked up the other and was shambling down the beach with it. But as far as I could see the whole projector kit was there. The M-D would come off duty that night, back to find his new toy . . . gone.

"Got the program disk too?"

"Of course," said Guppy. "It was underneath his pillow. And the box was on the table." She held up a plain brown box with a title pencilled on it: EXTERMINATOR Mk.10. Routine cyber-hero stuff, but it would do.

"This really gonna work?" said Maddog.

I'd reasoned this out once already. You know how they put on the air filters in the room before they show BeMovies? That's for the house dust, or the gestalt field draws it in and gets all grainy. Well, I thought, all we've got out here is dust. Or better, sand – sharp-edged, crystalline, glittering grit, as hard as the glass of the timeshare towers, only just not *organized*, not yet. What if we fed it to the gestalt field, so the image wasn't just energy and light, but matter: real hard gritty grainy stuff?

Actually, I didn't think it would work. But something would happen. There'd be a show of some kind. It would take their minds off me.

We lit a ring of small fires on the beach. There was fine sand here near the tideline, cool and moist enough to work with now the sun was down. It shaped up nicely; you could get real detail, down to fingernails and eyelids, all the fiddly bits. And we were working large. Ten metres off, the little ones were starting roughly on the golem's feet. Ten metres either side, big hands were coming. Maddog and I were putting finishing touches to the head.

I explained that the golem of Prague probably didn't look like Exterminator Mk.10 but Maddog wouldn't settle for anything less. You get a chance to build a hero, then you want the latest model. And a hero was what Maddog wanted, all the hero that a trashtype couldn't be.

"Straight at the wire," he breathed. "That's where we'll point him. Straight through." And he sniggered. Just behind the nearest stretch of wire there rose a smoked-glass Pleasure Dome. Glass on glass: it would make quite a smash.

"You sure the power cells will last out?" asked one of the others.

"Should do," I said. "Most of the energy goes into organizing the structure in the first place. But we've built the thing for it already. All it's got to do is get it up and walk."

Two, three hours later, we stood back and sighed. It was big, all right – twice the height of the wire. When the guards saw it coming, they'd be looking it straight in the knees.

We did a kind of chant, like in the story, walking round it one way, then the other. At the end, as we reached the word "life", I kicked the kid with the projector, and the BeTech generator jolted on.

There was a hush. Nothing happened. Behind us the waves slapped. Up in the timeshares there was laughter from some party, very thin and far away. Then nothing. Then, just as I thought it wouldn't happen, something happened. Something stirred.

You know when a crab burrows up through the sand, first there's only a mound, then it starts to take shape, then the sand crust flakes off, it stands up and walks away. That's how it was with the golem. It crumbled a bit from the edges, then held steady. It gave a sort of shudder, leaned up on one elbow, then got to a crouch, then stood up, just like you or me. Only twenty times bigger, that is, and muscular and armoured. Just, in fact, like Exterminator MK.10. It loomed up through the firelight and into the dark, so everything above the waist was lost to sight. For a moment it teetered, then lifted a boot and took a first step. Crash: the beach shuddered. Then another, then another, stomping out a bonfire like a dropped match. The trashtypes broke ranks and regrouped behind it, as it headed for the wire.

The guards didn't see it for some time, maybe because they weren't watching for anything like it. Then there was a howl of sirens and every searchlight slammed on in a dazzle bright as noon. There was a shudder of stun shots, then the rattling of hard ammunition, pings and whines as it glanced off the golem's glassy skin. Our hero swayed a moment, not so much at the impact, but as if it had forgotten something and needed to think. It was close to the wire now, just a silhouette against a wash of floodlight, but as I squinted after it the outline seemed to blur. I thought it was crumbling, that the power cells were failing but no, it was changing its contours slightly, still huge and still human, but there was something different in the way it moved and stood. Then I saw what was happening.

Maddog didn't see it. He was seeing what he wanted so badly to see: the trashtypes' vengeance marching on the timeshares, set to smash that cosy world to smithereens. The others saw it before him and one by one their cheers turned to groans, then giggles, then they whooped and laughed.

The thing was reshuffling itself on the move, as the Major-Domo's program took over, wrestling from inside with the shape we'd made for it. Of course! Would he have kept Exterminator Mk.10 beneath his pillow? I didn't think that was the kind of thing that turned him on. No, our colossus was blossoming out, getting curves where it had had muscles. The fists were unclenching, turning into long-fingered hands which lifted up above its head and swayed. Where the buckled belt had been, a snake-slim waist sloped down to sexy hips, that squirmed and wriggled. We had locked in part way through the M-D's program, at about stage four of the Dance of the Seven Veils.

"Guppy?" I said. "Did you know...?" But Guppy wasn't there to own up. Guppy knew how to look after herself; she had an instinct for it, like I said.

The guards' barks of warning faltered, turning gradually to whoops and growls and cheers as the golem finished its mutation and the giant striptease artiste took a last step forwards, jiggling mountainous above them as it slipped another veil. A helicopter, swiftly scrambled, veered around her, nearly slicing the wire in its excitement, and I could swear I caught a glimpse of the Major-Domo, running forward, eyes wide with fear and admiration, falling to his knees. Then Maddog realized, and he pulled himself upright and howled.

For a moment I thought: *that's it, now he'll kill me.* But the others had come thronging round us, laughing, pulling him with them. She was on the last veil now and they wanted to get right in close to see.

As they ran to the wire she started crumbling. All that extra power, going through the sex change, must have drained the power cells and she was going seethrough, grainy, blowing sideways in the evening breeze.

I didn't stop to say goodbye. With any luck, they'd have forgotten by next time they saw me. That's the up-side of these short attention spans. But Guppy was alongside, hop-and-skipping to keep up. I thought she was going to share the joke, but no, she wasn't smiling.

"Now," she said. "You owe me, remember?"

"Uh-huh." I was thinking of a nice cool drink and a sleep in the shade.

"It's Cazzie. My ma." Guppy grabbed my arm. "There's weird things happening. Weird and scary. Help me, Scip. You got to help me *now*."

Creeper: *Cazzie's Story*

1.

Listen. Can you hear it? That's the forest waking up around you. Green. A million pores are opening in a million trees. They yawn. They stretch. They sigh.

Feel the touch of a droplet of moisture. It likes you. There's a cloud that lives here, just beneath the forest canopy. Each afternoon it falls as gentle rain. The roots reach out to drink it up again. No, don't open your eyes. Sunlight touches your eyelids; everything glows green, green, green...

Stretch. Yawn. No hurry. There's nowhere to rush to. That was in the other world, the fast world, far away. Here it's your place in the sun. Spread out wide and feel it soak into your body, soft and slower than honey. As the sun gets higher, you bloom. You feel alive.

Don't move yet, but open your eyes. It's dazzling for a moment, there is so much green. See the veins in a five-pointed leaf like fingers, swaying just above you like a priest's hand saying: bless you, child, be happy, be at peace.

Isn't this what you always longed for, in the dry world, far away?

A bird screeches once across the clearing. No harm done. When a leaf falls it falls easily; it lets go. The ground catches it, gathers it back and in a week or two its life is rising through the root-hairs and into the veins of the tree, on its way to be growing, to be green again. To be green.

Just imagine. No struggle. Isn't this what mankind has always longed for, in the hard world, far away? Until now, only the mystics found it, or people in love, or else you glimpsed it in a dream and then woke to find it wasn't real. It can be real. Trust me. Breathe out. Sigh through all your pores. Be green. Be green. Be green. . .

Click. "That'll do," said Andromache crisply, clicking the recorder off. "Much better. That time you sounded as if you meant it." Then she smiled. "Good girl. As long as it meshes with the visuals from the simulation people that should be it. You can go."

"Oh," I said. "But . . . I get to see the movie, don't I?"

"There'll be no need for that," she said, dropping the smile.

The first time we met I'd been on my hands and knees in the upstairs corridor, scrubbing. Dr Andromache Spellman. I knew at once she was more than a guest. "Excuse me," she said crisply. I hadn't heard her: she moved light and fast, on high heels.

"Sorry, ma'am," I think I said. "I was miles away."

She stopped. "Say that again."

"Sorry. I mean, I was daydreaming, sorry. I'll get on now. Please don't tell the Major-Domo. I—"

"Child, child..." She was suddenly soothing. "I won't breathe a word. Just say it: *I was miles away*. Like you did. Soft, dreamy. That's it..."

"I ... I was miles away."

That was the voice she wanted, she said. For a special assignment. No, she knew that I wasn't professional, not a real voice-over artiste, just a grade E domestic in a timeshare, but... There'd be some cred in it for me. Well, I didn't wait to check with Boris. Only that morning we'd been worrying how could we score the cred to keep Guppy in clothes, now she was growing. And here was this topdogger woman looking down at me – I couldn't stop staring at her stockings, real silk, and her sharp-tipped shoes – looking down and saying "Just read the script, that's all. I'll pay." I always have believed that things come to you when you need them. Boris used to laugh, but this time I could say: you see!

What was I doing? I did wonder, just for a moment, as I followed her outside after late shift. They're into some weird things, these upstreamers with nothing to do with their time, particularly the ones who hang round Nefertiti's Tomb or the Zoo. Watch yourself, Boris would have warned me. Take a knife at least. But I don't think like that. I try to, but it doesn't come naturally. Maybe that's why we didn't work out, me and Boris, in the end. He's in Security.

There's a shrubbery in the courtyard. It's the real thing, under tinted glass, and *no one* is allowed to touch, but she beckoned me into the shadows and we sat on the damp earth under the dark green-smelling leaves. "Take a deep breath," she said. "Think, if the world was like this, all over..."

I started to laugh. "That's silly—" but she reached up and caught hold of a branch. "Hey, no, you can't!" I said but she bent it, very gently, till the end leaf touched my cheek. Then my eyes went blurry, I was sniffing like I'd got an allergy, except it wasn't, it was tears. I never told Boris, he'd just have laughed, but I often got these dreams, you see, with flowers in them, hillsides full of yellow flowers blowing in the breeze.

"That's what we need," said Andromache. "Real feeling. That's why I don't want an actress, I want you."

"Another thing," she said, as she brushed the tell-tale earth from my apron. "Not a word about this. Not to *anyone*. I'll pay." She'd buy my voice first, then she'd buy my silence. When your account's as empty of cred as mine was, and a child to feed, you say "Yes" to most things. The odd thing was, in this case, I'd have said "Yes" anyway.

"On second thoughts..." said Andromache. It had

been a month since the recording. Sometimes I thought it hadn't really happened – just one of my dreams. I never saw Andromache. She'd be attending to the business side of the operation, she'd said. "Things to do, people to meet, you know?" But how would I? I got back to scrubbing.

First time she told me it was a promotion thing, not a real BeMovie, I was disappointed, but she gave my hand a squeeze and looked straight in my eyes. "What these people will be buying," she said, "is worth more than that. It's the best thing on earth. You'll see."

"On second thoughts. . ." She went straight on from where she'd left off, weeks earlier. It was as if she expected me to be there, right where she'd left me, waiting. In a way, I was.

"Yes. We've got another job for you," she said. "Now I can be sure that you're . . . discreet."

"Of course. I've never breathed a word, honest. . ." It was true, too. Not a word to Boris, not to anyone.

"I believe you." She narrowed her eyes. "The job I've got in mind. . . It would be one evening. That's all. But this time it would be live and for real. The people who'd seen the movie and liked what it was selling, they would want to be there in the flesh. Don't worry," she said. "I'll write the script, you just put in the feeling. And after, you forget it, understand? Whatever you've heard and whoever they are." I nodded, meekly.

"You've got a little girl," she said. I hadn't told her. These upstreamers have their fingers on all kind of buttons, they can access all the data banks. "You're fond of her, this. . ."

"Guppy." I looked at the floor. The name sounded stupid, talking to Andromache. "That's what we call her. Guppy."

"Whatever," she said. "Keep mum," she smiled icily, "and there'll be an annual contribution to young Guppy's credit account. If not—"

"I'll do it," I said quickly.

"Good," said Andromache. I was glad I hadn't let her finish, though I couldn't think of a worse threat she could come up with than: *she'll spend her life working in a place like this, like you.*

"Now. . ." It was the night of the big show. "What's your name?"

"Cazzie. . . No, sorry, I keep forgetting."

"Don't. Tonight you are Calyx. Tonight you have grace, the artless grace of Nature. A child of the forest, the earth-mother's favourite daughter, right?"

I nodded.

"The game plan," she said, "is like this." A flicker of patterns appeared on the face of her micro-organizer. A couple of clicks, and she zoomed in. It was a room with chairs and tables. By each chair was a name. "It's the most compatible plan we could come up with," said Andromache. "Taking account of all we know about their biorhythms, pheromones, all the personal data. That much we can do with technology. After that it's up to us. Here's the schedule."

The pattern flickered away, and there was what looked like a script for a video, marked in fifteen-second intervals: here Andromache enters, fade forest music, hint of birdsong, waft of moist earth perfume, sound of running water, fade that. Then she speaks.

The micro-organizer went into voice-mode at a touch: Andromache's voice, word perfect, as it would be on the night. "So far," it purred, "all you have seen might be a dream. An ancient dream, true. To re-enter the Garden of Eden, where the lion lies down with the lamb. To cut free from the food chain with which evolution binds us all in bloody competition with each other, species against species, man against man."

There was a brief dramatic pause: *five seconds*, I read on the schedule; *establish eye contact with key clients*. "A dream? Yes, until now. You, here tonight, are the privileged few, the first to be privy to the secret: the technology exists! One simple DNA transfusion, by a process newly patented by my own research team, and every cell in the human body can begin to produce chlorophyll. Now all life forms can share the miracle of photosynthesis..." *Pause*, said the script, *for question, probably Table Three*. "Photosynthesis:

the process by which plants derive nourishment straight from sunlight. Sun – the inexhaustible resource – the only thing that nature, in this world, still gives us free."

"Consider the lilies of the field. They toil not, neither do they spin. Yet Solomon in all his glory was not arrayed like one of these."

Andromache was in action, and the small room with its small but most important audience was very still. This was it, the big night, and she was a born performer. I peeped from behind the giant indoor plants. She had her audience at her fingertips.

Table One: a tall woman leaned back, very thin, very stylish and without a hint of a tan. In the half-light her face had a glow like the moon. Her high Persian cheekbones had the look you get from a millennium of aristocratic inbreeding or a plastic surgeon and a bucketful of cred. At first you'd think *she's beautiful*, before you thought of skulls. The three men with her looked like athletes in suits. When she nodded, they nodded; when she smiled, not often, they smiled too. Lenore, warrior queen of a small data empire, was there with her current team of husbands. Her suit, purple satin so dark it was practically black, was straight-cut, all-in-one, so simple. It said, louder than any amount of show: here is a woman who could have *anything*.

Table Two: some folk with a high rating, Market Research told us, on the Religious Feelings scale. That bit about the lilies of the field, out of the Bible, that had been for them.

Table Three was different. Two adults — anxious, tense as schoolkids in a final lesson with exams next week — and two children, a girl and a teenage boy, looking puzzled and bored. Middlestreamers, folks who had some cred because they'd scrimped and saved. Now they were considering the biggest investment of their lives. Ms Table One sat as if she owned the place; they looked like it was a favour they were allowed to touch the chairs at all. Every now and then the woman nudged the man to ask a question, but he never did.

The kid on Table Four yawned, got to his feet and walked out.

Andromache didn't bat an eyelid. "Don't worry, I know that one," she'd told me in advance. "Calculated risk. He's in BeMovies, sort of. A bit of a star."

Think, I might have met Ivo Maccaby, in person! But I didn't. He left. The door-guards stepped aside to let him through; the door hissed shut. "Some people," Andromache went on without a hesitation, "might think all this is fashion, mere cosmetics. A new style aid." She glanced at the door, no more said, but I could see the others thinking: spoilt brat. She'd turned his little scene to her advantage. "No," she said.

"What you are witnessing is a way of life. A step in evolution. But..." she paused. "But there's a question. I can see it in your eyes. You're thinking: they can do anything these days with BeMovie trickery. *Is it real?* you'll be thinking. *Where's the proof?*

"Ladies and gentlemen, let me introduce Calyx, our first experimental volunteer."

I parted the leaves of the dragon plant and stepped into the spotlight. There was a gasp. The make-up team had worked hard; the shading was very subtle, like real suntans were, back when people actually tried to get them. I wasn't just green. There were shadowy parts, hints of myrtle around my eyes, between my collar bones, while my arms and shoulders had a wash of mint, like swimming under-water in a green-tint pool.

"Touch her," Andromache said. "She's flesh and blood ... and more than that, of course. She's real."

When she'd first told me what I had to do, I'd had doubts. It didn't seem quite honest. "Anyway," I'd said, "why me? Why not one of the real volunteers? There *are* real ones, aren't there?"

"Poor little Calyx," she'd patted my hand. "Don't get cynical. Of course there are real ones. They just don't look the part as well as you. Use your head..." she was back in business mode abruptly. "We've got an experiment to do, who do we use? People who won't be missed. The first round of subjects were trashtypes, naturally. They're fine," she'd said, catching my frown, "just fine. Just . . . not as pretty as you. Then there's your voice. That's unique. . ." No one had ever told me anything about me was *unique* before, not even Boris. I'd closed my eyes and let the make-up people do the trick.

Now, on the big night, I hardly heard what I was saying. Andromache had written it; I'd learned it word for word. How we'd gone to a special peaceful clinic inland. How the operation had been safe and painless. How, on the third day, this deep peaceful feeling rose up inside me like the sap in the veins of a tree. It was beautifully written, and it flowed off my tongue – all but one moment. When I got to the bit about the children, I had to stop and swallow. How we watched our children playing, safe and peaceful, in the forest glade. . .

In my mind I saw Guppy, not playing mug-tag in the binyards but lying on soft grass, not looking up, just counting petals on a daisy. That was the thing, not the daisy but *not looking up*, not glancing round, on the lookout for danger. For a moment I could see her *trusting*, like she couldn't trust this world, or anybody in it, even me. It caught in my voice. I cried a little.

"Good girl," Andromache said afterwards. "That was the moment. Natural timing." All I know is that when I blinked and looked up several more people were crying; others were clustering round me. I felt cautious touches on my bare arm, shoulder, knee.

Then they were all round Andromache, asking questions, signing things, accessing cred accounts.

Lenore hadn't moved. Her eyes were on me, steady. Not a word said. That's the thing about the rich. It's not so much the cred, the clothes, the smart technology – it's all the timespace round them. Me, I speak when I'm spoken to, come when I'm called. *She* speaks when she want to, *if* she wants to; if she doesn't, there's a silence. Everyone around her waits. Imagine that!

One slender hand uncurled, one slender finger beckoned, with a sharp nail painted silver. Not a word said, but I came towards her as if she'd pulled me on a string. She looked me up and down, she turned me round, the way she might calculate a bid for some new corporation: *yes, we could use that, lose that section, downsize, streamline but, on balance. . .* She nodded. Yes, she'd buy.

The middlestream couple got their turn with me at last. They were all over me, anxious, coming up too close. "It's such a lot of credit," they said. "But it's for the children. We've got to be sure." Too many questions. Andromache steered in quickly to introduce her business manager, who would talk about payment in instalments on easy terms. And that was it. My role was over. I could go now. I drifted back to where I'd made my entrance, through the dragon plants.

"Please, wait a minute. . ."

It was the boy of the family. He'd not said a word when I'd been with them, but stared at the ground looking sullen and sulky. Now here he was suddenly, stumbling after me, blushing. "The . . . the woman said we could touch you," he said and made a grab for my arm. I flinched; he pulled back his hand as if stung. "I'm sorry. . ." He blushed deeper. "I mean, please. . ." As I held out my hand he touched it, very lightly, once. His palm was sweaty. Poor kid. How old was he? Two or three years younger than me, maybe? I thought of Guppy. She seemed older than him, less innocent, though she was only five. He had the thing I would never be able to buy her, not if I saved for ever. He had had a sheltered life.

"I . . . I'm Henry," he said. "I thought it was stupid, all this Green stuff. I mean, Mother and Father, they've been going on about it. How it's our big chance not to be stuck in dead-end like them. My sister Melia, she'll do whatever they say, but I want to think for myself. . ." Suddenly he looked me in the eye. "That was till I saw you," he said. "If my parents can afford it, if they go ahead with it, will I really be . . . like you?" Behind him, I saw Andromache looking at us from the crowd. She nodded.

"Will I be able to . . . to see you?" he said.

It was over in an instant. Speaking Andromache's script for her was one thing. This was different, looking him straight in the eye. If I said *Yes* now, it would be a real lie. And I did. He wanted me to say it so much, even if it wasn't true. Perhaps somewhere deep down inside I still hoped that it *was* true. "Sure," I said. "I'll see you in the forest."

"You clinched it," said Andromache later, "whatever you said. They were wavering, that family. I thought we'd lost them. Then suddenly it was yes, sign on the dotted line."

"Andromache?" I said. "I've been thinking. Me and Guppy..."

"You'll get the payments, of course."

"No," I said. "I want to *really* volunteer."

"What?" she said. "Oh, no. That stage of the operation's over. We're in business now. All our subjects can pay. I mean, *pay*. Besides," she said, softening slightly, "you're too involved." So that was it. I'd been within an inch of the dream; I'd felt it brush past me; I'd *been* it. And now? Thank you, that will be all. I could go.

2.

Years passed. How many? It's hard to keep track here at Psylicon Beach. There's no change in the seasons outside, and inside the timeshares sometimes we switch season several times a week. They've got smart operators on the ambience machines these days, more and more clever illusions to flicker up on these bare concrete walls that are drying to powder, crumbling at the edges day by day.

The one sure thing was watching Guppy grow. She was out more and more – said she was in the staff crèche but I knew she sneaked off with the trashtypes out beyond the wire. I tried to tell her: kids like that aren't *friends*. With trashtype-instincts, anyone could smell that extra bit of cred on her, because Andromache kept her word: the payments kept on coming. But I was working most hours; what could I do? I never caught her out of bounds, though, so I guess she'd learned one thing that would come in useful in the real world. She'd learned how to lie.

Boris moved on, of course. It was the months after the Green thing ended did it. "What's the matter with you?" he'd say. "What's going on in your head?" I'd stare out the window at nothing at all. "OK," he said one day. "Who is it?" Because I was mooning, hopelessly, like you do when you're in love. And in a way I was in love, though not with *someone*. It was the thought of the forest, green light shimmering, the feeling that, at long last, this was really *home*. How could I tell Boris? So I went on staring and he'd shout till Guppy would start wailing; then he'd stomp off to the bar.

Getting old comes on fast when you're poor. I've seen domestics go from being young girls to old women overnight, then they go on being old for years and years. I'm not a quarter the age of most of the guests, these trim topdoggers on their young-for-ever trip, but I was shrivelling, I could feel it. I worked. What else was there? I worked my way up. Same job — cleaning, dust-sucking, chambermaiding — but I moved on from the Sherbet Fountain to the Kubla Khan and finally the Freestyle. That's *up* in the world, the most expensive timeshare on the Beach, for the few who can afford their own illusions, all different, not your ordinary package deal. Every suite is private, secret. Even the Major-Domo might not know quite what goes on inside.

Domestics know. We see things, we can't help it, and we're paid not to say. I'd had practice at that, thanks to Andromache. I stopped having those dreams, the ones of green light flickering and Guppy, or a younger Guppy I'd never get back now, playing on the forest floor. Dreams like that, you wake up crying, and what good's that? I'd done nicely for myself and Guppy, as well as you can hope for in the real world. You could say that I'd made it. Which meant I had things to lose.

The thing with plants is that seeds can lie for years under the earth, in a crack in the concrete, waiting. Then, a drop of rain falls and without warning they break through.

I'd worked the late shift. I came off duty and I was hurrying back to my quarters, to make sure Guppy was in. We're not meant to use the inner courtyard but it's a short cut and if you know the guests' movements like I do you don't get caught. Besides, I like to stop there sometimes, with the real trees. They leave green lights on all night, dimly, under-water in the lily pool, so the shadows go upwards, right into the sky. That night there were stars, real ones, not the ones they project there when the smog comes over.

There was a slight breeze, up from the creek, a whiff of mud and seaweed and the driftwood fires the trashtypes build there, sitting in a circle all night doing God knows what. The tree shadows shivered; you could feel they were alive. Then I froze. One patch of shadow, in one tree, was absolutely still. And it was watching me. The whites of two eyes peered out of the foliage, and where there should have been a face, there were leaves.

"Don't make a sound." The whisper was scarcely louder than the rustle of the trees. "Don't move. I won't hurt you." The leaves parted and it dropped beside me, landing silently. In the green light from the pool I saw a man's face, lean and bony, with shrunken-in cheeks, fringed now by tangled hair and beard. "Yes," he said softly, coming closer. "Yes, it is you. I've been waiting for you, Calyx."

"I . . . I'm Cazzie. . . You've got the wrong. . ."

"Calyx," he said again slowly, tasting the word like a gourmet tastes food. "Oh, I'd know you anywhere. With or without the green make-up." He reached out to touch me; I stepped back and slipped on the edge of the pool. In a quick flick his fingers fastened on my arm. It wasn't a hard grip – almost gentle – but I gasped, it was so strong. I could imagine those slender fingers tightening till the bones cracked.

"You remember . . . Henry?" he said. I could smell damp earth and crushed leaves on him. I nodded weakly. "Good," he said. "You should remember Henry." He smiled a thin smile. "It's OK, no hard feelings. You were doing your job. I knew it was a con, oh, as soon as we got to the Farm. Too late to change our minds then. My parents had paid up, and I felt so stupid. We'd already had the first injection, so the change was under way. You don't know about all that, do you?"

I looked at the face, distorted by the green light coming upwards through the ripples of the pool. The shadows deepened its hollows, so he could have aged half a lifetime. The tendons of his throat were tight with tension, like a creeper on a tree. Yes, it was Henry, but changed. I shook my head. "No, they didn't tell you much, did they? How they ride in the plant DNA on a virus. Makes you sick as a dog for a few weeks and by the time you come to it's in your system, spreading out from cell to cell. You can change your mind but you can't stop it then. Did they tell you what *that* feels like, knowing your whole body's changing, no, being changed into something ... something you don't understand?" I could have said: *yes, well, any mother knows that*. But I didn't. "No," he said. "You don't know the half of it."

Suddenly the grip slackened. "You've got to help me," he hissed. "You've got to. You owe me."

"Owe you?"

"Yes, owe me. For tricking me out of my life, my whole damned normal life. Oh Calyx, Cazzie, whoever you are, you owe me *everything*." He shuddered, and his fingers on my wrist were limp.

"What's the matter?" I said.

He shook his head, as if suddenly words were too much effort. "Come on," I said and steered him to the gateway. He leaned there for a moment, panting. "God," I said, "you look sick." But *sick* wasn't the word for it. In the white light of the EXIT sign, I saw that he was really, truly green.

"At the Farm, we were watched all the time." He lay back on my mattress like a felled tree. "The richest ones got five-star treatment, of course, private suites, but you bet they watched them, too. I thought it was just the doctors at first, running tests, taking notes. But even Andromache was all *Yes-Sir-No-Sir* with the observers, you could tell they were really important. Government, at least. At very least."

"What about the other ... subjects?" I coaxed another spoon of sugary ginseng pep-you-up between his lips. "Didn't you talk to them about this?" He flinched but he let it go down. With each dose a little strength came back, and as the strength came back he talked. He talked as if he'd talked to no one he could trust for years.

"Talk? Them? Most of them live by the poolside, just lying there soaking up sun. Just like most of them did *before* they got greened, only now they can make an entire lifestyle out of it, I guess. Lilypadders, that's what we call them."

"We?" I said.

His eyes flickered. "There are a few of us..." he said. That was all.

"Lenore?" I said. "What about her?"

"Oh, she's crazy – the kind of crazy people go when they've got everything. From the start she was into this religious thing, renunciation, fasting in the desert. Then she met Ukiyo, you know, the first Green astronaut..." I shook my head. "That figures," he went on. "That's what the government people were after at first, but hush-hush. Generations of astronauts, living up in orbit, feeding off the sun. They changed their minds when Ukiyo came back. He'd gone all mystical. Him and Lenore, they wanted to start this Zen monastery in orbit on the other side of Venus. That's one of the effects. Lots of Greens go poetic and dreamy. A bit like you...

"Sorry, sorry." He gave a weak grin, then his forehead furrowed. "No good for *action*, is it? That's when the government people twigged: there were other advantages, from their point of view." He closed a fist tight on a bunch of sheet. "All of a sudden there were secret delegations there from India, China, most of South America – get it, all the places with a population problem. They were thinking: hey, that's handy, makes the people cheap to feed, just water them and stand them in the sun. And they won't answer back, because it makes them peaceful... Most of them, that is."

"How do you know all this, if it's so secret?"

For an answer he held up a hand. He flexed his

fingers, long and powerful as the tendrils of a climbing plant. "Straight up walls, no bother," he said. "And quiet, too. I got all round that clinic, eavesdropped on their offices. Why do you think my code name's Creeper?"

The door clicked open. Guppy. In the struggle to get him inside, I hadn't even noticed that she wasn't home. I whipped up the sheet across Henry as she walked in. "So-o-orry," she launched off, her usual routine. "I was round at Mina's and... Ma? What's that?"

"It's ... it's none of your business. You're late..."

"Ma, it looks like a body!" Beneath the sheet, the green man groaned. Guppy smirked. "Ma-a-a," she said, almost as if nothing had happened. "I was going to ask you. There's a party in the next block. I could stay over..." She gave me a meaningful look.

"No. I mean, oh..." She had me, and she knew it. "OK. Just this once. And don't think it's because..." But Guppy was already gone.

Henry pulled back the sheet and looked round. All at once I saw the place the way it really was. Cheap servants' quarters. Just a storage space for low-cred people. Bare walls. One end cleared for the BeMovies in which Guppy and I tried to lose ourselves, night after night. And what kind of mother was I?

"Code name?" I said, changing the subject.

"Green Resistance," he said. "Angry Greens. Not all of us go placid, not when we see how they're going to use us. Some of us know." He flexed those long fingers again. "We could be strong. Cazzie, we need you. Are you with us?"

I looked round the bleak small room again. "What good would I be?"

"We think there's a party of lilypadders in this timeshare."

"I don't know. I mean, I know most of the apartments, except... I've not been on the top floor."

"The top floor? With the sun roof? That's got to be them."

"Who are they?"

"I don't know. Lots have passed through the clinic in the last few years. But if they're living in Freestyle, they've got plenty cred. We need it, urgent. We've got to buy some heavy weapons."

"Hold it," I said. "I'm on your side of course, but..."

He gripped both my shoulders. "Listen. When you found me, I was on my last gasp. I'd been two weeks inland, in the mountains. You know what it's like up there. Or maybe you don't. This place, it's an oasis. All the land between here and the city, that's desert. No shade, no cover, except the odd boulder. They had patrols out all day, hunting for me, so I had to move by night." He flopped back, limp. "You fade quickly when you need the daylight."

"You still eat, don't you? I mean, food."

He flinched. "Sometimes. But it gets hard. A bit

disgusting. You think of all that stuff mashed up and rotting down inside you, when you could just lie out in the sun."

"I'm going to make you some porridge," I said firmly.

He shrugged. "If I eat it, will you help me?" I looked down at him, lying there. Was I sorry for him? Was I guilty? Somehow it didn't apply. Yes, I'd got him into it, into this life ... but that was Henry, spotty, sulky, spoiled kid. That was someone else. This was Creeper, green man, revolutionary, hero... And he needed me.

"Yes," I said. "In the morning." Which was hours away.

3.

Lolene, with the grey bun and the old cough from Creek fever, had the top-floor duty. They'd be paying her extra for it, with the extra secrecy. But I'd done her favours; she owed me. Still, she narrowed her small eyes and looked at me.

"Oh, them," she said and shuddered. "The Garden set. They gives me the creeps."

"Just this once," I said. "For an old friend."

"Suit yourself," she said. "I'll call in sick this lunchtime, say you're standing in for me. And no..." She held up her hand. "Don't tell me why you're doing this. If there's anything peculiar, I'd sooner not know."

There was a tray of drinks to go up: no food, just tall frosted glasses full of multi-coloured fruit saps cloned from what had been the jungles of the world. When the lift got to the next-to-top floor, it stopped. On the last flight of stairs, there was a drinking mate of Boris's, from Security. He checked me with Personnel Central and nodded me on. As I climbed, he leaned against the bannister, looking up my dress, and whistled. The ice in the tall drinks trembled, but I didn't throw them at him. Strange, the thought of doing that wouldn't have occurred to me until that day.

On the top landing I glanced around. I listened. Then I put the tray down, marched to the window and eased it open. A minute later, long green fingers reached in silently. He must have been waiting outside, clinging on to the tiny cracks in the concrete facing, nine storeys up, not doubting I'd be there to help him. Trusting me.

As he climbed in I noticed: he was trembling. The skin of his forehead was glistening with sweat and pale grey-green. I wanted to hold him. Somehow I'd just assumed he would be fearless, but he wasn't; he was better than that, he was brave.

We didn't touch or speak. There had been time for that. Now it was time for action. Holding my breath, I tapped the compu-combination into the door pad and waited. It slid open. We were in the Garden, and thick scents of greenery and blooms hung in the air.

There was nobody there. I followed him, tiptoeing through room after room of lush shrubs, hanging vines and tendrils swaying in an artificial breeze. Broad leaves screened the windows like a forest glade. The carpet was springy and I bent to touch it – grass, not the parched straw you get around the Beach, but moist and thick and succulent. We could have been in Andromache's BeMovie, but it was real. All it needed was a baby Guppy playing on the grass, and it would be my dream. A hidden sprinkler hissed on for a moment, misting the leaves; a few drips sparkled on their tips. Somewhere further off there was the tinkle of a running stream.

"Roof garden..." Creeper pointed. Half hidden by shrubs was a small stash of the gardeners' tools, a billhook, a hose, secateurs, and a wrought-iron spiral staircase. "They'll be making the most of the midday sun." He turned to me. "Go back. There might be trouble." *No*, I thought. *No, there couldn't be trouble here*. My dream had been real all the time, and I'd thought it was gone for ever. When I was down on my hands and knees scrubbing the ninth-floor washroom, it was just above my head.

"OK," said Creeper. "But stay out of sight." He was up the spiral stair without a rustle or a creak. Then he stopped. I crouched behind him on the top step, and I saw.

The Garden set spread out round the poolside, or were floating on round pads of gently rippling foam. They could have been a Hollywood house-party from some antique soap, except for their clothes, those weird green frills and flounces draped around them like flightless wings. Then I caught my breath. No, all the guests were naked, and those were not clothes.

Creeper let out a sigh. "God," he breathed. "I didn't know they'd gone that far..."

The nearest body to us stretched and yawned. The

sleek skin of her back must have been Afro when she started; now it was deep glossy conifer green. She rolled on to her back and I clutched Creeper's arm. She was shaped like a greyhound, with a deep pit where her stomach should have been. "Don't look," Creeper whispered.

"But, but what happened to her?"

"Even at the clinic, some of them were getting into plastic surgery. Andromache tried to discourage it."

"You mean, she had that *done*. It's horrible."

"To them it's beautiful. The best money can buy." He was so close his lips touched my ear and his arm was round my shoulder, but suddenly he could have been a thousand miles away. "Cazzie, dear. You don't know how different they ... how different *we* are."

I shook my head. "But *that*! I mean, you..."

"I'm still on food. I try to keep my options open. These, they're total – sunlight only. Once you don't need to eat any more, a lot of things look different. You start to think it's ugly, having all those useless tubes inside. So they have them removed. That's just the start. Then there are the extensions..."

A cape of green spread out around the greyhound woman, like the petals of a huge exotic flower. It shaded from light green at the fringes smoothly to the laurel of her body, where it joined on seamlessly. "Folds away when she's not basking. In the stomach cavity. You see?" His voice was suddenly cold. "I told you to go back. You still can... OK, have it your own way." He was up on his feet, coiled, then he leaped into the sunlight. "Freeze!" he cried.

There was no panic. No one started or jumped to their feet. They looked up slowly, one by one. A man with a sun-catching frill like a tropical lizard cocked his head to one side. "Hey," he drawled. "What's rustling you?"

"Green Resistance!" Creeper started. "Brothers, sisters, we've been passive long enough. It's time ..." He trailed off. One of two of them had looked away and gone on basking. Someone giggled. "Look at you!" yelled Creeper. "You call this a life?"

"A life? Sure." The lizard man chuckled. "I call this *the* life." The others watched, still sprawled or drifting. I had an awful vision of them being carried from place to place by porters. Could they move at all?

"What's your problem?" purred the greyhound woman.

"Don't you ever think what's happening out there – in the real world?"

"Think?" said a woman with a shaved head and skin flaps from thumbs to waist like bat wings. "Where did that ever get you? What I think is, we've got just exactly what we need."

"Vegetables!" Creeper paced among them. "That's what you are."

"Correction," said the greyhound woman. "Not that

it's an insult. But I'd see us more as orchids. Hothouse flowers."

"Great!" scoffed Creeper. "Who's in charge of the greenhouse?"

"Why, the Guardeners, of course," said the bat woman with a glance at Lizard-Head.

"Quite so," he said and for the first time moved his right arm a few centimetres, to a small remote control. "I think he needs the Guardeners." And the whole place jangled with alarms.

The five figures who crashed through the doorway weren't Greens, not under their visors and uniforms. They were Security. Creeper reached in the bag he had slung on his back and whipped out a blade like a machete. It glinted as he backed into the full glare of the sun. The sunlight must have given him energy, because suddenly they were coming at him and he was hacking and whirling as if he had twenty arms. One, two, three of the guards went down in the blur, then he was spinning round to face another, but the last – it was Boris's mate from the stairs – slipped in behind him. With a dull thump, Creeper toppled forward.

"That's better," said Lizard-Head. "He was beginning to disturb us. Now we can get on with the business." And he stretched out in the sun.

"What shall we do with this one?" said one of the Guardeners. The other gave Creeper a poke with his boot.

"Not dead?" drawled Lizard-Head. "Better see what you can get out of him about this Green Resistance business. See if there's any more of them around. Then weed them out."

Creeper groaned as the guard grabbed a handful of hair. He dunked his head fiercely face down in the pool. He held it there a moment. When he yanked the head up, Creeper was gasping. "Now," said Lizard-Head. "Talk? No?" *Splash*. The guard rammed his head down again. And again, and again.

"This is no good," said Lizard-Head. "He's protecting someone. Make sure you don't drown him till he's told us. Put him downstairs – in a nice dark hole."

A blast of water caught the guard in the small of the back. It was only a garden hose, but just enough to trip his balance. As the guard topped forwards, Creeper twisted sideways and was on his feet. *Splash:* the guard came up gargling, shouting, but the other wasn't listening. He'd whipped round to face the sudden shrieks as small running figures came leaping out of nowhere, screeching and laughing. Trashtypes, swarming. And you, Scip, shouting orders, and... Yes, there was Guppy, whooping as if all this was the best game she'd had all week.

Lizard-Head was wobbling to his feet. There was a slash, a billhook; green blood splashed. Trashtypes were flailing round with garden tools and lassoos made of vines. "Guppy!" I screamed, as trashtypes spread out, laughing, ripping plants down, looting anything that glittered. Some were dunking the first guard underwater again and again, getting carried away, so they forgot the other, the man from the stairs. He was bringing up his blast gun, setting it to close encounter mode. How did I know this? I learned some things from Boris, things about Security. "Set those things to short range, widest angle, highest power," he said, "and you'll jelly anybody's brains in sight."

Then Creeper lunged. He got the guard's arm, wrestling him backwards, back to the rim of the roof garden, twisting the arm up till the bone went with a sudden crack. As the gun spun away into space, the guard crumpled, pulling Creeper off balance, and the two hung there, for a long, long moment, on the edge. Then there was a long scream. Maybe two.

There was a flapping of skin, a feeble weeping, as the lilypadders gathered up their grotesque bodies, waddling and tottering as the riot went on round about. There was Guppy beside me. "You shouldn't. . ." I was saying. "Bad girl, bad girl. . ." The usual words, the scolding-Guppy words, came out, by habit, but she put her arm around my shoulder. "Sorry, Mum," she said, "I couldn't just let you go off by yourself. And Scip knew what to do." I looked at the edge of the roof garden, but she held me back gently. Then I let her hold me as I cried.

* * *

"What am I going to do now?" said Cazzie. Strange how people always thought I knew the answers, though they were grown up and I wasn't.

"What's the problem?" I said. "No witnesses — the trashtypes saw to that. The whole thing was hushed up. Who wants bad publicity? And everyone knows that riots happen, bound to. That's the way it is."

"That's not what I mean," said Cazzie.

I was missing something. Don't forget now, I was just a kid.

She took a deep breath. "How would Guppy feel if I told her she was going to have a brother or sister?"

"What?" I said.

"Creeper. . ." she said. "That night. He was strange, but. . ." She looked up, with a strange look in her eyes. "But beautiful." And I felt my skin prickling slightly. There was something in the world I hadn't picked up on the Beach.

"I . . . I guess you'll ask for bigger quarters."

"What if it's different? I couldn't stay here with it, could I?" She gazed out of the window. "It might not fit anywhere, much."

There was a bang and Guppy swept in off the street. She looked at me, and at Cazzie. "You're not doing words again, are you?" she chirped. "You should get out on the streets more. Get a life!"

"Guppy?" Cazzie called after her, but she was gone already. Bang: the door shut. "Where's she going?" Cazzie said, then smiled weakly. "I know, I know. Probably gone to get a life."

Wildcatting

1.

Dead quiet in the Outer Lots. Nobody on the streets, not even a stray cat moving. Here and there you saw it chalked up – on a wall, a paving stone, the peeling blue side of an empty pool: BOYS N GIRLS CUM OUT TA PLAY.

Back inside their security fence, the timeshares were doing business as usual – faint muzak, sounds of muffled parties – but out in the Lots was this hush. Not normal, not normal at all.

A summer night, still hot as the sky cooled through orange and purple into blue-green. Nights like this, you'd get streetlife, trashtypes out on rooftops, laughing, plotting, playing strapjack, trading the day's goods, settling scores. You'd get fires on the beach and smells of something barbecuing, don't ask what. But not that night.

One small figure, moving through the stillness. Guppy. Moving fast.

The Outer Lots were a world of their own – abandoned plots, empty pits for foundations, streets trailing off into dust. All these buildings that planned to be grand. The walls had a hacked-off look. It could have been a film of a war zone but no, nothing that exciting ever happened here. The tides of the holiday biz washed the big cred somewhere else, just when Psylicon Beach was getting geared up for a boom, and all the building stopped.

The lots weren't empty, though, oh no. There were more people here than in the timeshare blocks, except there wasn't a guest list and if there was it would change every week. Once in a while, Security mounted a raid for stolen property or unauthorized dealings that were getting cheeky, interfering with their own. By the time they arrived, and it could just be minutes, all they found were empty cellars, scuffings in the dust that could be rats, and a feral cat or twenty that outstared them with eyes like blank video screens. They'd bulldoze the whole place flat, they used to say, if they could afford it, and Psylicon Beach would be a real top-notch destination once again. Dreams: that's the stuff the place was built on.

Some nights I'd look at the reflections of lights in the Creek and I'd imagine I could see them, all the mega-leisure-domes that never got built. All the people with leisure-lives so busy they need an on-line console to remind them which pool they'll be by next week. All their cred. Or maybe I didn't imagine it. Maybe it's what Psylicon Beach did, like a middle-aged washout dreaming of the things he might have been. Dreams were its business, like I said.

Reflections, breaking up in ripples as I drifted in to shore. By the time I touched shore she was waiting. "Hi," she said and I could hear that she was out of breath. "Where've you been? I've been looking everywhere for you."

"Hi, Guppy," I said. I could feel that stillness. "Does your mother know you're here?"

She must have been trying to stay cool, to sound me out first, but she'd been holding on to it too long. "They've got her," she blurted.

"What?" I said. "Who?"

"Security. They've got her in Sick Bay. Locked ward."

"Slow down, let me think." It didn't figure. Working for the timeshares usually all it took was one slip, one cocktail taken to the wrong table or two minutes late, and you were out on the streets to take your chance among the trashtypes. If you got sick, well, it came to the same thing. If a guest got sick, of course, there'd be room service. No, Sick Bay was something else, not so much Health as Security. And a *locked* ward...?

"She's not sick," Guppy said. "Not yet... Scip, they're giving her drugs, mind treatments. I think they guessed about her ... her and Creeper. They want to find out everything."

She looked very small in the twilight. She was just a

kid after all. "How do you know all this, Guppy? Sounds like classified info to me."

She squinted through the gloom. "Scip, you're with me on this, aren't you?" I nodded.

"OK," she said. "Follow me. I want to introduce you to my dad."

Through the wire, in the dark, he looked like any other guard. We walked straight up to him. "Scip, this is Boris. Dad, this is my friend Scip."

"I'm putting my job on the line, you know that," he muttered. "But, heck, I feel sorry for Cazzie. She always was a bit weird, of course. It's this place, it does it to you, if you think too much." He lifted his visor an inch. Just his lips showed, a glint of his teeth, uneven at the front like Guppy's. "Listen, kids. Leave the dreaming to the guests. They can afford it. Types like us. . ."

This was not time for fatherly advice. "Which ward?" Guppy said.

"SB30.6. There'll be a guard on each door. Best chance is this: most of them smoke buzz-weed. Can't do that in the Sick Bay. They're not meant to, but every hour or so they'll step outside. It takes about five minutes to light up and get through a toke, so you'll have to move fast." He came up close to the wire. "If they catch you, not a word about me, OK?" That's when I noticed the sound, coming up from deep under the unnatural quietness, like a soft pulse beating underground. "That's it," Boris muttered. He hinged down his visor and was just a guard again. "It's starting." Then his personal bleeper went dingbats, flashing Red Alert.

"What's starting?"

"The Wildcat. You two, get lost, fast!" As he spoke there was an eruption. Back across the Lots, where floods had carved a cleft beneath a concrete forecourt, trashtypes poured out, stamping and yelling. Tonight, of all nights, just when we needed to be cool and think: a Wildcat! And it had begun.

No one issued invites to a Wildcat party. The authorities always said there were ringleaders, but I'd never met one. It was like tides, just the pull of the moon and the wind from a certain angle, and whoosh. Maybe that was what happened to the world, or all the world I've seen. It wasn't always like this. One big tide came in and stayed.

Guppy told me about her first Wildcat, once. Cazzie had told her, like good parents should, to stay inside. Don't move, don't look, but she went to the window herself and started staring. Guppy was a toddler then; she could only just reach the handle, but by the time her mother turned round she was out of the door. Outside, she could see the Security guards from behind, all lined up along the wire as something crashed against it, hard. As she peered through the legs of the guards she thought the earth had split open and all the monsters had been let out – men with horns or fangs or feathers or with two heads or two faces, one grinning, one crying, looking either way. It didn't help when a big trashtype kid pulled off his mask and flashed her a grin with gappy teeth. By then she was wailing, but as soon as the carnival moved off round the perimeter – they didn't break through that time – everything seemed sad and empty, so she set off to follow it, biting her lip. You know Guppy; she's been like that ever since.

Across the waste ground now, the first wildcatters hit the street. I mean, really hit it. Some of them were running, others dancing, tumbling, walking on their hands. Most of them had drums, at least a can, a dustbin lid, a hub cap. The ground trembled. Suddenly there was a heave and a cheer and it clattered out into the open, the centrepiece of all this, the Big Cat. *Wham* – the noise hit me as it jolted into sight, and four or five fire dancers leapt out spinning torches, devil-sticks with flames at both ends, juggling balls of fire.

Cat doesn't describe it – that's just short for Cata-lyser. Think of a carnival dragon, as long as a house, but built from old oil drums, twisted metal, ripped-out cables. Think of it creeping caterpillar-like on any old wheels ripped from wrecked cars and trucks and kiddies' push-carts, anything that rolls. It had ribs, that was for certain, hoops and struts of bent steel, but inside the body its heart and its lungs were amplifiers, speakers, banks of bulbs and wires and coils. At the rear end, for guts, there was a generator, a petrol-filled antique, older than Psylicon Beach itself, and it shuddered and chugged. Now its light circuits jolted into action, flickering in every colour. It moved with the crowd – you couldn't see who was pushing, who pulling. The thing had a mind of its own.

That's no joke. No one controlled the Big Cat. Yes, the trashtypes built it, slightly different every time. By the end of the party it would have shaken itself to bits. And kids took turns to ride it, just for the thrill and the risk. It broke limbs sometimes, and it shattered ear-drums. But no one told it what to do. The Catalyser had this biofeedback gizmo in it, plundered from some clinic long ago. It picked up the pulse of the party around it, heartbeats and brainwaves and what not, and it amplified and speeded them up some, then a little more. The drummers and dancers would speed up with it, rattling their pans, clapping, stamping, clanging bits of metal. Suddenly the waste ground was a surge of people, scenting the rich-pickings smell of the timeshares, making for the wire.

"Scip," Guppy whispered. "What about Cazzie?"

BOYS N GIRLS CUM OUT TA PLAY. . . Back in the old days, the flare-up would have come about now. As the first of the party animals caught sight of the lights through the wire – the floating glitter-globes at the

poolside or the flicker of projections on a curtain –
they'd start a low growling cheer. It would build to a
chant, slow and menacing: PAR-TY TIME, PAR-TY
TIME... That was back in the days when folk still got
angry at the gap between the worlds, the world of
dreams and the world of scuffling and scraping by – a
gap a light-year wide, though they were no further
apart than the thickness of wire.

BOYS N GIRLS CUM OUT TA PLAY. WE'VE
COME TO BLOW YER MINDS AWAY. The first rank
of Security were lined up with their visors snapped in
place. They probably couldn't hear the chanting but
they'd be getting edgy. If they couldn't hear the party
they could feel it in their bones. Any moment now the
dancers would reach frenzy and start leaping, jump-
kicking the wire, twanging back into swaying out-
stretched arms; they'd crowd-surf a while before
balancing upright to leap again. At each clash there'd
be a roar like a big wave breaking, and the tide of
people would keep coming till the fence gave way, and
there'd be kids scattering into the gardens as the
guards lashed out around them with their riot sticks.

That's how it used to happen, and there we were
now, pressed flat against the wire, ready for the first
heave. But it never came. Instead, the gates swung
open and everyone was streaming through. The
Security men were looking on like bouncers at a night
club, *nothing to be scared of if we're good kiddies,*

right? As the Big Cat dragged itself into the mall between the Fountain and the Kubla Khan all the windows were lined with faces of guests, watching. That's what we've come to, these days, in Psylicon Beach. Just part of the show.

TRICKORTREAT, TRICKORTREAT, TRICKOR-TREAT… It was the old words, passed down for centuries, kind of a ritual, though they got a bad name just pre-Millennium when kids started doing it with guns and baseball bats. Windows were opening now, and guests tossing out trinkets and sweeties with chemical centres, small consumer goods, upstreamers' cast-off toys. Someone launched out a glitter-foil streamer, and some of the bolder guests were climbing out in fancy dress. They must have spent a lot of cred to look like trashtypes for the night.

That's when the new chant started, one I'd never heard before. It went ZOO-ZOO-ZOO, WE'RE GOING TO THE ZOO-ZOO-ZOO…

The Zoo. I knew about the Zoo: the most secretive of the timeshares – except for Nefertiti's Tomb, that is, but who wants to know what they get up to there? You caught the sound of it sometimes: a Howler monkey screaming the dawn in, or the champing of a leopard on its kill. Guests in the other timeshares exchanged glances and reassured themselves that it was only virtual. Which was more or less, but only more or less, true.

The whispers came back through the crowd. "They're inviting us in." "Free!" "Yes, all of us." "The Big Cat too."

It was crazy.

"It's that new Mixer they've got..." Suddenly everyone in the crowd seemed to be clued up. "You know, new girl from the city, she really is crazy. She's mixing things there like they've never mixed before."

It's all in the mix, as the old proverb has it. Could be the motto of Psylicon Beach. Every last little fantasy, somebody's had it before, but it's the way some artist sits at the console and weaves it: the projections, the music, the scent-taps, the mood-enhancing sub-liminals and the things they slip into the drinks. They're artists, these Mixers – MCs, DJs and con-jurors all in one. I'd heard rumours of this new one from the city: *Metanoia*. She was into high excitement. Risk. One of the guests last week, word had it, went home in a body bag. All hushed up, of course, but word got out. And oddly enough, business had been better since then, much better. The Zoo had been slipping – had to boost its ratings somehow, so they were going for a high-risk strategy, employing her.

"There's a party going up there," went the whispers. "Hundreds of them, all gone virtual together."

This was new. When I was small I couldn't help imagining that there were real animals in the Zoo. That's what zoos were in the olden days, before people started thinking it was cruel. Besides, things were going extinct, even faster than most people realized. Folk jetted halfway round the world to see the last tiger in Pyongyang till one day the 3-D projector broke down and they realized it had been a hologram for years.

These days you don't go to see a tiger. You go to *be* one ... virtually. You get your own cage and a head-set, and when you plug in, suddenly you get the eyes and ears and senses of the beast. You can prowl, and electrodes feed your movements back into the pro-gram, so you see the jungle moving round you, and maybe you start feeling hungry, and what's that? A deer? The howls and snarls that leaked out from the Zoo some nights weren't sound effects. They were rich kids acting out their hunts and kills. In other words, a big adventure in a padded cell.

But a hundred of them, all gone wild together, no cages? It had never been done before.

"Metanoia's calling for the Big Cat," went the whispers. 'Reckons that'll really get the party going."

"There'll be a riot," I said to Guppy, and for the first time that night Guppy grinned. Then I thought: Sick Bay was just beyond the Zoo.

The Big Cat was struggling on the wide flight of steps up to the main doors and everyone set to, shoulders to whatever wheel they could find. The beat slowed to a heave – grunt – heave – grunt – heave.

The noise of the party already under way inside the Zoo came down the steps to meet us. The two beats hadn't meshed yet, but when they did. . .

At the door of the Zoo two guards stopped us, big beef mountains of men. "Where you going so fast, tadpoles?"

"Metanoia," I said. "Got to see her. . ."

They exchanged a grin. "At your own risk, tadpoles. She eats squabs like you for breakfast."

Black on black, that was the first thing I saw. Black walls, black seats in the alcoves of a long black hall. Some of the clients sat twitching like dogs in their dreams as visions of African plains unreeled inside their bulging fly-eye goggles. More, though, were up and moving, ducking and weaving in and out of things nobody else could see. There was a pounding throb, nothing you could call music.

Two virtualizers lurched towards each other in a kind of slow-mo blind man's buff. You could see the moment when it happened: their programs picked up on each other, their illusions meshed and each turned into something in the other's dream. One leaped back, her arms up in a pose that deep in her brain might be a Bird of Paradise spreading its wings to fly, shrilling alarm. As I turned, a thin girl reared up hissing and out of the corner of my eye I saw her head haloed by a cobra's hood. When I looked straight it was gone. That shouldn't have happened. I wasn't wired up to anything, but I'd seen what I'd seen. There were spooky things happening all over, a flash of a wing or the slash of a claw, that couldn't be really there, but. . . What if there was feedback? What if bits of things leaked out of one virtualizer's circuit into the next? Or worse, if they got lost in between, wild dreams taking shape by themselves in the air? Had Metanoia thought of that? With a lurch I thought: *oh yes, she has*. There'd be BeProjection gear rigged up all round the dancefloor, catching stray thought waves and making them real. Metanoia was nobody's fool. She was brewing the party to end all parties. And the Big Cat hadn't made its entrance yet.

There was a rumbling growl behind us. I spun round and there was this dark shape crouching. It was a guy in black, broad on the shoulders, but there was something in that crouch that told me here was a boss-male mountain gorilla, even though the things had been extinct since the turn of the Millennium. Over the glittery goggles, you could just see a greased quiff of Elvis hair. "Duckhead! What are you doing here?"

"Hi, Scip," he growled. "Some party!"

"Duckhead. . ." I was being careful. How do you chat to a guy whose every sense is telling him that he's a boss gorilla? "You can see me?"

"Sure I can see you. I can see *everything*. Hey. . ."

For a moment he stared out into vacant air. Over the heads of the stumble-dancers smoke was rising, flickering with strobes and lasers. "Look out!" With a bat of the paw that felt somehow twice the size it actually was, Duckhead pushed me and Guppy aside and was up on his hind legs, swiping at the air.

"Frigging airplanes!" he roared.

"Duckhead!" I yelled. "That's *King Kong*. You've got interference from some movie channel."

"What? Oh ... yeah..." Duckhead shook his quiff, gave one last swipe and shrugged. "Hey, you seen Metanoia? What a woman!" He pulled up close with a whiff of authentic gorilla sweat. "Special friend of mine."

"You know her?"

Down at the dark end of the hall the mixing desk was raised up like an altar, with a face above it, gleaming darkly. "Me and Miss Metanoia," Duckhead nudged me. "Miss Niagra, that is, we go back years."

This was our chance. "Take us to her. She could help..."

"Hold it," growled Duckhead. "The lady's *working*."

Guppy grabbed Duckhead by the cowboy-buckled belt. It was as high as she could reach. "Please!" she wheedled, as cute as she could. "I've lost my mummy..." Duckhead pulled himself upright, all ready to pound his chest when something in the program reminded him that gorillas looked after their young. He stared at the crowd and gave a roar. In the split second everybody froze and looked, a way through opened, and he pushed Guppy into it. "Go find her," he growled, "little one."

With a jolt like the pre-shock of an earthquake the Big Cat lurched into the hall. Virtualizers staggered as the rest of the Wildcat crowd poured in. Both sound systems missed a beat, then locked on each other. For a second it was like two stray cats meeting in an alley; eyes wide, a twitch of the tail... Then the two beats crunched into synch and the swivelling lights were meshing, twisting round each other in mid air. Where they crossed, the visions, just a flicker in the corner of the eye before, were taking on colour and physical form. I ducked and wove, trying to keep up with Guppy as wild things, real and unreal, swooped and tangled round our heads.

Metanoia. She was up there on the mixing desk, riding high. She was bent over the console driving it like a trucker on a non-stop to the city, roaring through the night, and her face was gleaming with the lights and dials. She might have been Cazzie's age, but as compact and strong as Cazzie was willowy-thin, as glittering black as Cazzie was pale. She was magnificent. "Hey, squabs," she called sideways through the shuddering beat. "What's your problem?"

"Help us," Guppy shouted. "They've got Mum..." She climbed up and yelled in her ear.

Metanoia nodded slowly, not taking her eyes or her hands off the deck. "Yeah," she said slowly at last. "I got a problem with this place, too. Let's shake it. . ." She threw a switch. As total feedback howled from everyone's virtual circuit to everyone else's, the atmosphere burst like a zigzag of lightning, the BeProjectors went into overdrive and the crowd was swamped in all each other's dreams and fears.

There were the animals, of course, leaping into the spaces between them, as good as real. Just beneath the console a panther looked up from her prey, and the buck she'd been mauling craned its head, and its eyes were the eyes of the little smart barman from the Sherbet Fountain, always flirting with rich women for a little extra cred. Then the big paw came down; he was meat. *Don't look*, I was thinking, *it's just virtual*. I was following Duckhead, fighting his way forwards through the crowd. As he squeezed past the kill, I slipped and went down, in a pool of real blood.

Duckhead roared. Around him, jungle creepers parted and the worst fake dinosaur I'd ever seen came trundling at him. He didn't care: he was King Kong now completely, and he reared up, pummelling his chest. The rubbery Godzilla clumped by, shaking the floor, and something shrieked. Beneath its foot there was a heap of blood and feathers, shuddering once before melting back into the body of a virtualizer, a real topdogger, really dead. In a second, a trashtype from the street-party outside stood over him, ripping off the bug-eye goggles and the headset and ramming them on to her own head. As her street-dreams locked in there was a bellow, and the Big Cat reared up on the hindmost pair of many scaly legs. A long lick of dragon flame crisped the wings of a low-flying Pegasus that crashed down, tons of horseflesh, through the smoke. Somewhere up in the rafters, flames were taking hold.

"Hey!" Metanoia's eyes were shining now with pure glee. "Who's putting out the ancient history stuff?" That was just as I made it through to the console. She squinted at me and looked as if she was going to laugh, then looked again. "Yeah," she said. "It's you, isn't it? Where do you get it from? Fall of the Roman Empire... Just the stuff we need!" She slipped a headset on to me, neat as a game of deck quoits. "Dream it, brother!" Metanoia cried.

The walls shuddered. A great iron-braced gate with tree-trunk bolts and hinges had appeared from nowhere, bulging and splintering a little with each thud of a battering ram. Once more, and it burst; the barbarians poured in, howling out for pillage, and behind me graceful marble columns tottered and the domes of old Constantinople shivered like a shipwreck. All the stories I'd heard, all the pictures and statues and ancient-world junk in the Tower was taking shape around us, and it had a mind of its own. Then the real doors crashed in, and there was Security, hacking their way through the Viking berserkers, Zulu spearsmen, a huddle of terrified fairies and the mayhem of everyone's dreams in the Zoo.

By the time the first guard forged through the console, Metanoia was already on her feet, up on the console, laughing. "Get down," she called to us. The guard lunged. Metanoia kicked the volume switch on full and a Malibu breaker of raw sound seemed to lift her up, right off her feet. The arms of the crowd went up and caught her, surfing her hand to hand, just as the sound wave hit the Big Cat and it reared up, sparks all round it like a coat of flame. Then it exploded. There was a moment of eerie silence, then everyone was staggering, panicking, battling to escape.

"Don't forget Cazzie," shouted Guppy. "Bring the gorilla!" By the door, lit by flames in the smoke, we found Duckhead. "Kong," I yelled. "Fay Wray's this way..." That's when I tripped on a crocodile, which disintegrated into heaps of coloured stones and sand. In the midst of them sat a wiry wrinkled brown man with a fuzz of beard and a most puzzled look on his face. The crowd that had banked up behind me surged forwards, carrying us out into the night.

There were two guards at the Sick Bay, both sprawled on the doorstep with their buzz-weed smokes in hand. "Hey, strong stuff..." one slurred to the other. "I could have sworn I saw a gorilla." We could have just asked them for the keys, they were so out of it, but Duckhead barged the door down all the same. Most of the patients were at the windows cheering, looking better than they had for years. In a side room, Cazzie looked up at us with a vacant drugged smile. "Hello, dear," she said. "Is it visiting time?" She frowned a little when Duckhead hoisted her on to his shoulders, then decided this was just another dream. Outside, we ran.

The party was breaking up. Fabulous creatures plucked from way back in everyone's brains were going see-through and thinning like smoke. The freak storm of energy that had brought them into some kind of being was over and as we scattered they winked out one by one. In a while we were just a lot of trashtypes running, some clutching fragments of our precious Big Cat, heading for the Outer Lots where we belonged.

2.

The Outer Lots were deathly still again. We were getting our breath back, stretching out on a flat roof staring at the stars. Cazzie shivered a bit, as if the sedatives they'd given her were wearing off. She looked around, blinking, taking in the fact that this was real.

"As for this lady," said Duckhead. Virtualizing over, he seemed to have shrunk back to normal size. "She matters to them. Why?"

"Guests..." said Cazzie in a slurred voice. "I ... know things ... 'bout people ... 'portant people... Ssspecially those Greens..."

"So why didn't they just off her?" said Duckhead, impatient. "Back where I come from, folk get vanished every day."

"You sssee..." Cazzie shook her head. "They know about me and Creeper, and..." She patted her belly gently. I glanced at Guppy. She just looked at her mother a moment, then laid her small hand over Cazzie's. Duckhead frowned, still puzzled. "Fancy..." Cazzie muttered, "I'm a sssperiment."

"Whatever," said Duckhead. "There'll be search squads out to find her. Better get her underground."

"I know a place," I said. We went, keeping our heads down, just in case of night-sight scanners. We were within smelling distance of the beach, at the top of the low cliff, when we heard the sound.

It was like a machine, throbbing and humming, but less regular. It ebbed and flowed, a bit like breathing, but it never quite stopped for a new breath. The nearest thing was a huge cat purring, but it was hollow and echoey too, and as we came to the edge we stepped out on a concrete slab and felt it through our feet.

CALIFORNIA SURF SHACK – OPENING SHORTLY. Someone had slapped up the sign back in the days of big plans but the building never got much further than a roof and floor. Since then the Creek had eaten back the cliff, and the Shack was a sandwich of reinforced concrete hanging halfway up the crumbling slope where land crabs scuffle most nights. Most slither back down again and again, but once in a while one makes it to the top and ends up on some timeshare's menu. Not that the guests would touch it if they knew.

I looked at Duckhead and Duckhead at me, a silent *after-you, no-after-you*. Cazzie was shuddering now; she needed shelter. We slid down a little gully till we could scramble across to the lower slab of concrete and we perched there, peering into eerie dark that growled and droned and hummed.

Then it stopped. Just like that, with a dry huff and a ringing in the air. I could just make out a shape in the glow of a fire.

Something was squatting there. For a moment it was a fly, almost man-sized, with its legs crooked up around it and black wings and a long proboscis. Then it was a man, cross-legged, with his shadow stretched behind him, and the long snout was a length of broken down-pipe he'd been playing like an instrument. He looked up – a dark crumpled face, a fuzz of white beard – the little bushman from the stampede at the Zoo.

Nobody moved. The small man crouched like a wild thing cornered. Then Cazzie did the right thing. Very slowly she sat down on the concrete, cross-legged, just like he'd been. One by one we did the same. The man relaxed. With a *that's better* look like a teacher when the class has just stopped fidgeting he turned back to his pipe. He pumped up his cheeks till they gleamed, about to pop. The drone started again.

On the bare concrete floor was a pattern, too big to make out at first, traced out in sand and shells, crab claws and pebbles: a more-than-life-size spiky crocodile, just like the one at the Zoo.

"Wow…" Cazzie breathed out in a long sigh. "Crocodile Dreaming… That's the stuff they used to do, oh, centuries ago, in Australia."

"He's got to be virtual," Duckhead muttered. "Some weird thing from Metanoia's show."

"No, he's real." I knew he was. I've got an instinct for these things. On the walls behind him, the old Australian had scratched out shapes, black and white, with beach chalk, I guessed, and a charred stick, like an ancient painting in a cave.

There were hills in the painting, and a desert, cracked and parched as land round here. No roads or buildings. There was an outcrop of rock and people gathered round it, small black stick-cartoons, and in the sky an arc of spirit creatures: Crocodile and Platypus and Kangaroo. They made a circle together and there in the centre of it, last of all, was a crack, a great crack through the heart of that world. In the crack, forcing it wider, stood the figure of a woman, huge and black, an earth-goddess at the very least. Her arms stretched out towards a tiny figure – him with his fuzz of white beard – as if to pull him through. The woman, you can guess, was Metanoia.

How long this went on I don't know. All I remember is the whanging growl of the didgeridoo, and the way – was it the firelight or the way your eyes go when you stare too hard? – that all the creatures in the painting seemed to quiver as if they were trying to wake up and come alive. One moment it was dark outside, the next there was dawn in the sky.

With a last whoop and growl, the old man laid his pipe aside. He was up on his feet, advancing with stiff ritual steps towards the painting. As he got closer so his shadow shrank as though it might just fit the picture of him on the wall. He stepped up to the crack in the heart of it all, and leaped, as if one bound might take him through.

Crump. He stuck there on the wall an instant, then he gave a little grunt and crumpled. By the time we reached him he was already struggling to his knees, beating the wall with his bare fists. But it was only concrete and it wouldn't open. "Poor thing," said Guppy. "He wants to go home. He can't get through." Everybody turned to her and stared.

"What's with this *own world* stuff?" said Duckhead. "Either he's real or he's virtual, right?"

"She's right." It all made sense, though it was crazy. "He's real," I said. "But he doesn't belong here, not like here and now. You saw the things that were manifesting last night? Things from way back, myths and legends? Where did they come from?"

"The Dreamtime?" whispered Cazzie.

"People always dreamed of a place like that, as long as there've been people – somewhere all the things you can imagine really are. People always thought that maybe you can get there, if you get enough power together – that's why they had rituals, dances, chanting. Maybe you can step through, right from Then to Now?" Everyone looked at the Australian, still slumped with an awful lost look in his eyes. "All this, the cave paintings, the music, he was trying to get enough power. Last night there was plenty."

Cazzie came to the lip of the concrete and gazed out at the Creek. When I looked her eyes were filled with tears. "He can't go back," she said softly. "Like us. We can't go back either, you and me."

"Let's get out of here." Guppy was practical all of a sudden. "Duckhead, you got a truck?"

"No chance," Duckhead said. "That's the first place they'll check. There'll be guards on the exits. You can't just vanish like that. . ."

"Oh, no?" I said. "What about Metanoia? Where do you think she's got to? If anyone can do it, she can."

The old Aboriginal squinted his eyes, looking up the bare chalk hill. There was less of that lost look about him now. He was tracking again, he was reading the signs of the desert, doing what he was best at. "Ah!" he said suddenly, and loosed a torrent of words in his own language. But I recognized the last word, let out on an awe-struck sigh: "Metanoia." And he pointed, unmistakably. *She went that way.*

We looked where he pointed, up where the parched grass ran out on the stony hillside. There was a dry gulch, cut by the flash floods than ran off the hillsides every year or two. If someone made it that far they could be out of sight of the timeshares right to the horizon. What was beyond there was anyone's guess.

The way to the city was by truck, like Duckhead's. Setting out to walk there was a thing you didn't do.

Was it a blade of bent grass the Australian noticed, or a scuff mark in the ground too slight for us to see? All I knew was, I took his word for it. Metanoia went that way. Duckhead grinned. "I've had enough of trucking, so. . . Whaay-ell, if we can catch up with her, I reckon we can have ourselves a bit of fun. You want a thrill, there's no better place to be than with Miss Niagra . . . sorry, Metanoia."

"Us, too," Guppy chirped up. Then she frowned. "Wait here. Got to say goodbye to someone." Before anyone could speak she was running back down the hillside, raising a trail of dust as she went.

I caught up with her just outside the timeshares. The place looked as if a tidal wave had hit it. The stampede had lifted a whole stretch of fence and carried it a hundred metres before the wire snapped, leaving coils and tangles tipped with wicked barbed wire. They must have been picking up bodies from first light but, even trying not to, I spotted one or two more where they staggered into ditches, losing blood. Trashtypes. Even in the body-bag business it would have been clients first, the ones with holiday insurance.

There were no guards to challenge us. We just walked in. There were huddles of guests, watching wide-eyed, not quite sure they liked this show. Most had packed overnight, and were waiting for the company to rescue them, though the thought did strike me: why would the company do that? If these people got home they would only sue.

In a last-ditch grab at tranquillity, the management had turned up the background track of woodland streams so loud that the birdsong was like sawmills working. The aromatherapy department had let rip a billow of soothing perfumes till the guards in their visors started to cough and choke. In business terms, this was disaster. It might have been a desperate PR stunt, but there was a whisper that the Major-Domo at the Kubla Khan had ritually disembowelled himself on the patio.

Round the back of the staff quarters, we bumped into old Lolene. Her eyes flashed – maybe warning, maybe fear. "You just stay out of sight," she hissed at Guppy. "You and that damn-fool mother, bringing troubles on us all. You was always sneaking off. I should sneak off for good, if I was you."

"Don't worry, we're going," said Guppy. "With Metanoia."

Lolene slammed down her bucket so a precious drop of water slopped. "Don't mention that name. . ."

"What do you know about her?" I said.

"What does anybody know about your Metanoia! Or whatever she's calling herself." She poked her broom towards us like a riot stick. "Only that she's a top-rank anarchist. You know that? Half a dozen other timeshares she's played tricks like this." She cast a sly glance upstairs, where Cazzie's room was.

"They're looking for you," Lolene said. "Scoot, while you've got the chance. And take your trouble with you."

Guppy led the way, round through the binyard. I could hear the Security jeeps in the street out in front of the quarters, but she found us one of those holes in the fence that no one but the kids would know.

With a scrape and a wriggle we squeezed through the hole, and came up . . . face to face with the metal-tipped boots of a guard. His visor was down and I could see my own reflection gone all smeary in it as he bent right down to stare at Guppy. His walkie-talkie crackled: *Agent 257, please report. . .* He held the mouthpiece to his visor.

"Nothing to report, Chief, out OK." He clicked the off-button for a moment, and shook his visored head at us. "You going somewhere?"

"Better," Guppy said. "Hadn't we?"

He nodded. "Better," he said. "Good luck. And that Metanoia. . . Quite a woman, eh?"

Guppy stood on tiptoe and planted a kiss on his visor.

"Bye, Dad," she said. "And thanks. Be seeing you, one of these days."

The Big One

1.

I'd had a dream. So what's strange about that, you may ask? Well, real dreams are rare here on Psylicon Beach.

Did folk in the timeshares dream? If so their dreams came programmed. All part of the package, like ambient music and the filtered air. Not to mention the sleep-easy tablets that knocked you out before you had a chance to think. Yes, sleep was one of the things you paid for, with in-house security scanning your room, closed-circuit cameras watching over your bed like guardian angels.

Did trashtypes dream, out in the Lots? They slept in snatches with their belongings beneath them. If they were lucky they could huddle back to back for safety, if they thought there was anyone else they could trust. Trashtypes sleep shallow. If they had dreams they forgot them by the morning. Probably a good thing, too.

Sometimes, out in my Tower, I'd lie listening to the water and wonder if I was the only one who got a good night's sleep round there. But dreams? I tried not to.

The trouble with dreams was you'd start wanting them to come true. It took your mind off what was really happening. You'd lose your edge, and edge was all that counted. Without edge I'd be just another trash-type – in other words, as good as dead.

I'd had this dream, though, I couldn't deny it. I was diving, deeper than ever before. It was out in the heart of the Grey Stacks, in the dangerous canyons of the ancient Mall. It wasn't so much the toxins there – they were worst among the chimneys of the factories and storage tanks. It was the fraying wires and shards of glass that hid themselves in thin silt and could cut without you feeling, so the sharks got wind of it before you did.

In this dream the water was clear as air, the surface a bright rippling mirror overhead. I saw metal stair-cases and the cogs that moved them. I saw the signs and symbols everywhere and wondered why in the world should there have been so many? "Think of it as a temple," said Uncle Homunculus. "Different people liked to worship there in different ways." Ah, yes, Uncle Homunculus. He may have been crazy or making it up, and he's long gone now so I can't ask him. Uncle Homunculus taught me most of everything I know.

In some rooms in the dream there were clothes. Most had rotted but some were plastic and they floated from their racks of hangers, silt-grey now but still in rows. Here and there were plastic people, lying at all angles, almost lifelike but horribly thin. Some wore shreds of clothing; some were naked. Some were bald; some had arms or legs missing. Whatever had savaged them, I knew suddenly, would be coming for me.

There wasn't much time left. The more I panicked, the more I'd run out of air. I struck out for the exit, a revolving door. The glass was cracked and if I pushed it might just shatter, but I eased it through a quarter turn, and then it stuck with me inside it. As I looked behind there was a flick of a tail. Shark? No, it twisted lithely and reached out towards me, reached with graceful human hands and its face was a girl's, calm, curious and beautiful, like no one, trash or topdog, that I'd ever seen.

When the storm struck, it came without warning, like a punch a secret enemy's been saving up for quite some time.

I was at my narrow window in the Tower, looking inland. I'd done that a lot since Cazzie, Guppy and Duckhead left. Sometimes I'd catch myself wondering about them, then I'd come to and pinch myself. *Edge*, I'd say, *Scipio. Edge means here and now*.

That morning I could see the timeshares glittering like a mirage. Suddenly the air went thick and as moist as a steam bath. Then dark. The daylight shut off and the storm hit, wind and rain together, with a screech like a truck in a skid. Then the crash. I was lucky I blinked; every window went purple with lightning. A glass dome, Uncle Homunculus's favourite knick-knack, launched off its high shelf and smashed behind me, as if the wires and bones inside, once a stuffed owl, had a crazy thought that they might fly. In the top of the Tower, the massive bell called Great Ned broke its ancient silence: *donnngggg*. . . Like the springs and levers of the big clock everything was rusted, jammed. Now as the storm hit there was a shower of plaster and dust. It hung in the air and shuddered with the force of Great Ned's *donnngggg*. . .

By the time I got back to a window, the storm was moving away. I could see a slate-grey slab of cloud veering across the Creek, whipping up little water-spouts, trailing tentacles of rain. Behind it, the Creek was choppy, slapping to and fro.

All around, apart from that, the sky was blue, like morning, not the blank white glare it would be soon. No clouds. The storm was small and fierce and neat and it had come from nowhere. It wasn't the first that had come in off the sea that week.

"Freak storm?" Boris had said when I'd asked him. "No more freak than you or me. Well, me. . ." He glanced round. Yes, the other guards were out of earshot. He gave his helmet a *know-what-I-mean* sort of tap. "It's the boffins," he said. "Tampering, big time.

Seems they picked up the idea from that, er, accident with the BeProjector on the Beach, remember?" He leered, then went serious. "If it's true, soon they'll be making rain. Think of that. Few teething troubles, though, they say. . ."

After the storm had passed, a monitor plane came over high up, circled, then flew on. It's useful knowing Boris. You've got to be paranoid to work for Security. That kind of paranoia makes you hard to live with, just ask Cazzie, but it gives you an instinct for the way things really are.

Way out on the horizon there was a heat haze building, just like any day. In the haze another storm was waiting, and another and another, lined up at exactly equal intervals, ready for the word to go.

I ran down the stairs, to the sea-level balcony where I hauled the boat in. It was still there, swamped but OK. I glanced out again at the horizon. Three little fists of grey, still parked and idling. Who knows how soon they'd send the next one over? If I had any sense I'd sit tight in my Tower. But I didn't. I cast off the boat and slipped down into it. I had somewhere else to be. I had a date.

It was all of a week since I'd first seen her. At first I hadn't seen her at all. All I'd seen were fireflies playing on the water.

It was the end of a not-bad sort of day, making hit-

and-run raids on the fringes of a party. Young media tycoon-tykes, down here on business, celebrating some new project or deal. I was keeping my wits about me. Now the old Major-Domo was gone, his replacement was a new broom, busily showing the world that he wasn't a greedy self-serving bribe-taking placeman. Or in other words, he was open to offers. What they'd done with the old M-D, I couldn't find out. He'd gone downhill fast since the business with the alligator. It had shaken his confidence and he'd started in on the pills and the drink. Things got sloppy at the Sherbet Fountain. I guessed that Peaktime Timeshares Corporation had weighed up their investment, Courtesy Intensives and all, and cut their losses. Usually discards like him turn up in the Outer Lots, scuffling with the rest of us, but the M-D hadn't showed up yet.

So the new man was keen, and I had to make do with skulking in the courtyard, sidling up to people with the *wanna-see-something-really-old* routine. I'd shifted a small hoard of glass, a rack of last-millennium beer mugs, an ashtray with the words MURKEY'S IRISH STOUT printed on the bottom inside out, all but a few little trinkets, when the new M-D saw me and I melted tactfully away into the night.

It was dark by the pool, and oddly quiet with the fake waves and seagulls turned off for the night. The water was black and flat as a dance floor. Suddenly a swarm of fireflies danced.

Not real insects, of course. You get the cassette from Reception, if you can afford the remote control to play it with, and you can make them dance anywhere – in your bedroom, in the bath. . . The other model had Tinkerbell fairies. It was quite a short sequence, and I watched the pattern play itself out two, three times, before I noticed someone else was sitting at the poolside, quite still, just a shadow. Then she leaned a little closer and the flickering green glow picked out her face.

She was my age, more or less, as far as you can compare topdoggers' time with ours. Her features were narrow, rather long but fine, and white like the marble statue, Aphrodite, that Uncle Homunculus had got me to scrub clean of its mould and slime. As the fireflies faded for the fourth time, she reached for the Play button again, then hesitated. She looked up, suddenly aware of me.

I knew that face. The mermaid from my dream.

"Sorry," I said, "I didn't mean to. . ."

"Don't mind me," she said. "No one else does."

"Nice fireflies," I said lamely. "Are you . . . are you at the party?"

"Do I look as if I'm at the party?" Now my night vision came into play I saw how she was sitting, legs tucked up and cradled in her bare arms, head drooping a little. She brushed her pale hair back again from her face. She didn't look as if she ought to be out here alone.

"Shouldn't you be inside. . . ?"

"Sure. Dangerous out here. All kinds of trash-types, who knows. . ." She looked at me straight, then just for a moment her thin lips flickered in a bright surprising smile. "You sound sort of . . . different, for a street kid."

"I read," I said. "I've got books."

"Books!" She gave a little laugh. "I've heard of those."

"I've got lots of old things. . ." I reached for my bag. "If you're interested. . ." Then I stopped. I didn't want to go into the bargain-haggle-beat-them-down routine. It would be over too quickly. "My name's Scipio," I said.

"Chiara."

"Chiara. . ." Something came back, something from the Tower. "Doesn't that mean light?" She looked up, puzzled. "In the old days . . . painting. . ." It was coming back slowly. "Chiaroscuro. It means light and dark. . ."

She was watching me with her lips pursed in a doubtful sort of way. But she was watching. "Light. . ." she said after a moment. She smiled. "Light. . ."

Just then a door hissed open. Outlined in the doorway was a man. He was young, late teens maybe, but surely not a kid, a man. "Hey, Chi," he said in an easy drawl. "Come in and meet some people."

"In a minute." She didn't turn round.

"I'm saying," he said firmly, "that people are starting to notice." He took a step out towards the pool. He saw me.

"Well. . ." he said. "Who's your little friend? One of the locals? Quaint." He thrust a hand out at me, to shake if I dared.

"You like antiques?" I heard my voice and hated it – a street-seller's wheedle. "Genuine old glassware. Something for the lady. . ."

"If I wanted anything, trashkid, I'd already have it."

"Rocco!" She swung round sharply and her eyes were narrowed. "This is Scipio. We were talking."

I was already on my feet. "Er, I'll be going. . ."

"No!" she said. "Scipio was telling me about old paintings."

"Paintings!" Rocco laughed. He did it easily, like someone used to telling others just what's funny and what isn't. "We've got them in digital archives. All of them."

"Rocco," she said to me, "is Deputy Prime Exec of BeQuest Innovations. He'd like you to know that."

"Sure," chuckled Rocco. "And what post does Professor Scipio hold, may I ask?"

"Clear off, Rocco," said Chiara. Then: "Five minutes, OK?"

He didn't stop chuckling. He chuckled slowly, taking his time, as he went in. When he had gone, he left an awkward hush behind him.

"Uh, I . . . I'd better go," I said. "Sorry if. . ."

"No," she said quickly. "It was fine." She jabbed the On-button again. "That's just Rocco." And she sighed. I waited for more, but she was lost in the fireflies again. In profile I could see the neat curl, like old-fashioned handwriting, of her nostril, between lip and cheek. The fireflies went through their motions.

"You know what that spells?" I said. She looked at me sidelong, with a little wrinkle of the nose. "Each one flashes a sequence," I went on quickly. "Morse Code, you know, *dot-dot-dash*. . ."

She was shaking her head, but sort of smiling.

"Old world stuff," I said. "There's a chart on the wall in the Nautical Theme Bar. You can spell out letters. *Dash-dot-dash-dot, dot-dot-dot-dot*. . . That's C – H. . ."

"Quaint." She gave that little laugh. "So what are these little guys saying in Morse Code?"

"PEAKTIME TIMESHARES CORP. An advert." I took a step back. "I got to go."

"Where?" she said. "Do you really live . . . out there?" Out there, where she glanced, was the vague darkness of the Lots.

"No. I've got a Tower. Really. Out there in the Stacks, on the Creek. . ." She was squinting at me, half believing, wanting to believe me but losing it fast. I felt this sort of twinge inside. If she laughed, if she thought I was lying, if she turned and walked off now. . . What? I didn't know. This is me, Scip, the man with the plans. I'm never at a loss . . . or not till now. What was happening to me?

"Oh, come on. . ." She laughed, but gently. There was a din from the door. Not just Rocco, but several voices. Laughter. Big topdoggers' sort of jokes. She tossed her hair as if to get the sound out of her ears. "Tell me." So I did.

I started with Uncle Homunculus. No one knew where he came from, and when I asked him, the answer was so tangled up with stories from books he'd rescued or pictures or statues from the drowned museum that I never could tell which was which. I tried to describe him, with his blank white eyes like the Roman statues we found in the museum hall below. The statues were bald, too, and one had a name on it: "Scipio". Uncle Homunculus gave me the name when I came to the Tower. It might have been the toxins that got to his eyes, but he'd begun to realize they were failing. That's when he'd gone out to get an apprentice, a little trashtype not too bothered by a fear of water. That trashtype was me.

He told me a story once about the Tower. How this mad curator, solitary, eccentric, wouldn't abandon his museum when the tide came in. Like the captain of a sinking ship, said Uncle Homunculus and laughed. How this crazy man hauled as much as he could up the clock tower stairs and squatted there among it. He told it as if it was someone else – maybe an old man who had taken him on, too, as *his* apprentice – but I wonder. Something in the water does strange things to how we change and age out here. I mean, look at me.

She did, Chiara did. She looked at me.

Then she was scrambling to her feet. "Better go," she said hurriedly. "If Rocco comes out again, he'll kill you." She paused in the doorway. "See you," she said.

"Wait!" As she turned I held out on my palm the one thing still worth having from my hoard: half a little cutglass crystal, cracked off at a slant. Her eyes narrowed again. I could guess what she was thinking: *cheated; he's trying to sell me something after all.*

"No," I said. "Take it." The flash of anger faded. "Put it in a window," I said. "See what it does to the light." There were shapes in the door, too much in the glare to see us out in the dark. Without a look back she folded her fingers round the crystal and was gone inside.

2.

As soon as I pushed off from shore I regretted it. *Ssstupid . . . ssstupid . . .* the ripples whispered, like an old friend who's just got to give you good advice. *Should never have said*, it whispered. Telling my secrets to a stranger, mixing business with . . . what? I didn't know. I did know, though, like any trashtype, that giving anything away is danger. It's like handing someone else a weapon. Out in the Lots, being friends means knowing someone's name and where to meet them . . . and there I'd been, telling this upstreamer girl about myself, about the Tower, about Uncle Homunculus, about my dreams – all in five minutes flat.

Something had got to me, some new kind of toxin. I was losing my edge. And edge, like I said, is all that counts here. Don't forget that, Scipio.

Cut your losses, whispered the beat of my oars. By the time the outline of the Tower rose above me, with the round white face where old-world time (the kind that goes in circles) had stopped, bigger sea-waves were muttering the same advice. *Forget it, forget. . .* She'd been filling an idle moment, she hadn't been listening. She'd forget anyway, lucky for me. A spoilt topdogger brat, good riddance. Ouch. The boat jarred against the wall. Another lapse of judgment. I would have to watch it. And I did watch, half that night.

I'd keep an eye out, just in case she'd told Security. That's what I told myself. I'd have some warning if a launch was coming. But she wouldn't tell them. Would she? I watched the lights go down, the parties winking out like glow worms, and I wondered which one was the Sherbet Fountain. I wondered if Rocco was still laughing, and if she was with him now. At last, still propped up at the window sill, I dozed.

When I opened my eyes the Beach was dark, all but for one last lantern. It flickered, as if someone was walking with it through a glade of trees. *On-off-on-off...* A short flash then a long one. *Dash-dot-dash-dot...*

Morse Code.

...E – A – S – E...? Then a long pause. It started again.

C – H – I – A – R – A... it said. S – E – E – M – E – P – L – E – A – S – E.

It was an hour till first light. Then I'd push out the boat and go and see, just see. The waves were lapping downstairs, with more good advice, but was I listening? She'd remembered about the Morse. She'd bothered to find out. She'd remembered me. Chiara...

I was wide awake. I had to go. I had a date.

The second storm moved in so fast it came pushing a bow-wave in front of it. I'd just reached the edge of the Stacks when I looked round and there it was, coming in a smooth arc steered, I'd guess, by satellite. I rowed for my life. The air pressure thickened fast, I was running with sweat, but I got to the balcony, winched the boat up and lashed it fast. I slammed the door behind me and leaned back against it as *wham*, the wave hit. The doorframe shuddered, water sluiced in through the cracks around my feet and the Tower seemed to stagger. *Donnn*— went Great Ned, cut off oddly in mid-clang. Pause. Then the ceiling exploded, and the big bell splintered its way on down right through the rotting floor. There was a final dull *sploosh* underfoot. Through the hole, black water slapped and frothed and boiled.

By the time I dared move, the sky had lightened. I looked out. The sea had a bruised look, purplish-grey, but the seascape had changed. One of the Outer Stacks, a crumbling concrete shell with the letters UN ALLIANCE etched in it, had simply gone. As before, the wind dropped, just like that. There was a spattering of small rain this time, almost like the real stuff. Yes, I've seen it once or twice. Then I realized: of course, that's what they were after. Small local show storms are one thing but what they'd be wanting was a force of nature, strong enough to start the cycle going, sucking up water and feeding itself like real weather. They'd be going for the big one, and the next might just be it...

The horizon was blurry with heat haze. On it, the next-in-line storm cloud, surely a bigger one, waited. The boat was drenched but OK. I lowered it, water seeping from the gunwales, fast. It was crazy, of course. I should stay and sit tight. I stood more chance in the Tower than rowing. But I launched off. Don't forget, I had a date to keep.

I did well. I was gasping, muscles twanging, ramming the boat through choppy waters, rowing harder than I've ever rowed before. I didn't ease up till I was well up the Creek. Low spits of land were closing round me; the Beach was in sight. I leaned a moment on the oars and gasped for breath.

There was a landslide roar of thunder. Out by the Stacks, a slate grey backdrop had come down. Against it, lightning snickered from point to point; the Tower stood outlined black a moment, then the rain closed in. I didn't see what happened next, not clearly. A small tidal wave, fanning at a tangent off from the track of the storm, must have entered the Creek. Funnelled in, it grew higher; I just had a glimpse of it, a murky wall with a scummy foam crest beginning to break, as it blocked out the view. Then there was crashing and pummelling, greenish darkness and a dream of trampling crowds, fists pounding, ramming me down. Dimly I thought: *even a diver can't hold his breath for ever*. Some time soon I'd give up and be drowned.

I hit the sand as hard as falling on to concrete. It knocked out my last breath, but I stuck there. Foam was pouring back all round me with a get-you-next-time sort of roar. I lay there, flat out and spreadeagled, like sunbathers used to do on purpose in pre-Ultra-Violet days. My clothes steamed round me. After some time a shadow moved across the sun. *No, not another storm*, I thought. I opened my eyes.

The man was all in black – black long coat and black, very broad-brimmed hat. He looked at the other one, identical, beside him, and they nodded. They looked more like undertakers than Security.

"You the kid called Scipio?" said one.

"Sure he is," said the other. "Boy, you nearly missed your big appointment. But don't worry. We'll make sure you keep it now."

You didn't have to ask the way to Nefertiti's Tomb. It was always there, in the corner of your eye, at Psyli-con Beach. Most people made the effort not to notice it. Other timeshares turned up their ambient sound tracks, threw special late-night parties, anything, to cover up that certain hush that seeped out of that place.

On the outside it was nothing, just a concrete portal, vaguely Egyptian, set back in the hillside like the Valley of the Kings. If there was more to it than that, they kept it underground. You couldn't complain about it. There was no loud music, no revellers spilling out on to the streets, no unsettling night cries like you got from the Zoo. It was quiet and all very tasteful. A customer simply approached the portal and it would swing open. A couple of servants in the plain hemp shifts of the ancient Egyptians would spirit them off to a vestibule, where they'd exchange their business clothes for something more suitable.

Or so they said. I'd never been inside, or talked to anyone who had. I once knew a man, an ancient trashtype in his thirties, who was offered a job there. Good pay, good conditions. He couldn't say *no*. But that night he took all he owned and made a break for it. Whether he made it, or his new employees caught up with him, I don't know. No one saw him on the Beach again.

This came back to me as I stood there with my black-clad escorts, waiting for the gate to open. Slowly, heavily, stone hinges grinding, it did.

In front, a stone corridor sloped down out of sight. Some torches flapped sick-yellow smoking rags of flame, just bright enough to make the dark beyond look even darker. But a side door opened, silently. As the door shut behind me I blinked. No stone decor and torchlight here; I was in a comfortable office suite.

The first thing I saw was Chiara. She was standing by the window looking very slight and pale. She opened her mouth as she saw me, but she never got to speak. Rocco's voice boomed first: "Well, hi. . ." He shot her a look that said *shut it*, and she tightened and stared at the floor. Then he swivelled his chair to face me, smiling. "Oh, excuse me. Were you thinking: three's a crowd?"

On the desk he had one of those toys, metallic balls on wires and levers: when you push one it nudges another, nothing happens for a moment, then the next one swings. I kept my eyes on it and didn't answer. Everyone, I guessed, was like those balls to him.

He tapped on the table: *dash-dot-dash-dot, dot-dot*. . .

I looked at Chiara. She was staring at the carpet, her face very pale, lips very tight. "You told him!" I said. She mouthed *no!*

"As it happens," Rocco broke in, "she didn't. She would have, of course, when she'd finished her sulk. I didn't feel like waiting. I left a bug by the pool when I went back inside." He waited. "Oh, dear. . . I do believe you look relieved. You must be thinking: *she didn't tell on me, she likes me*. Didn't know you street kids had romantic feelings." He laughed, the same sort of sudden laugh that she had, only deeper, from the belly, not the throat. "Be careful, trashtype. Dangerous to lose your realism. Specially when it's all you've got."

Outside the triple-glazed window, behind Chiara, fronds of a hanging vine began to thrash about in silent wind. Even through the smoked glass I could tell the sky had darkened. Another storm was coming, even here.

Rocco noticed it, too. Swinging his long legs down, he paced to the window, letting his fingers graze my head as he passed. It was almost a pat. With the same swing of his arm he laid his hand on her shoulder and left it there. "Don't get me wrong," he said, looking at me. "You're no problem. Chiara here, you've guessed, is my intended. Cousin, too, as it happens. We're a tight-knit caste, us BeMedia types; we've got to be. Too many secrets – pays to keep them in the family. Chi and me, we've been lined up for each other, signed and sealed, since before she was born."

She didn't move or make a sound, though I imagined I could see her quivering slightly. Maybe it was me. A small trailer of vine tore off and tumble-weeded slowly downwind. Rocco squinted at it. "Odd," he said, then turned back to me.

"Don't try living in some last-millennium movie. Chi and me, we're one species, you're another. You can put that all out of your mind, because you've got another appointment." He savoured the pause.

"That's right. It isn't her. It isn't me. There's someone else who's been asking for you, old friend, most particularly. And at a moment like this," he beamed rather horribly, "people's requests do tend to get granted."

He waved a hand; the door slid open. In the corridor the two attendants were already waiting. Over their Egyptian robes one had a jackal head, the other one a hawk.

"See you," said Rocco as they steered me to the door. "Just be thankful you're indoors. Looks like difficult weather."

"Who's doing it?" I said quickly. Anything to prolong the conversation. I didn't much like Rocco, but faced with a choice between the Guardians of the Underworld and him... "These storms. Someone's BeTeching them, aren't they? Is it you?"

For the first time he didn't have an answer ready. "You're not stupid, at least," he said slowly. "Since you ask, yes, we *are* engaged in a small experiment. Thanks to BeQuest Innovations the weather round here might take a change for the better. You might even get a spot of rain."

"A spot? I nearly drowned."

He made a you-win-some-you-lose-some gesture. "We didn't reckon on anyone living out in that toxic rust-heap," he said. "Set that against the benefits. Rain. With its own mini-climate, Psylicon Beach could be green. A real oasis. Boom-time again..."

"And what about the trash kids in the Lots? That wind of yours flattened some shacks – I saw them. . ."

"That," Rocco said, "would be a public service. Do you think our clients like to see that kind of squalor? No, a good deluge might be just the answer. . ." He moved to a console where a map-like pattern flickered. Contours, windspeeds, isobars. "I might turn up the volume for the next one," he smiled. "No, just joking. It's a matter of fine judgment."

"Do you know what you're doing?" I said. The jackal man tugged at my arm, but Rocco raised a hand. "You've seen it. Don't you think I do?" he said.

"No. The first one was really controlled; the others, each one's been a bit more haywire. The stronger they get, the less they stay on course. And there's a high tide coming, you know that?" I looked past him to Chiara, but she didn't look up. I should have known better. She was helpless, broken somehow. If she hadn't spoken up by now, she never would. As if she'd forgotten about me completely, she drifted over to the weather console and stood gazing at it vacantly.

Rocco was nodding, thinking. "If that last one was a tryout," I said, "I don't want to see the Big One."

"Don't worry," said Rocco. "I don't think you will."

3.

Imagine a multi-screen cinema carved from raw stone. That's the decor we descended into. Under their fancy dress, the two henchmen were the same as brought me from the Beach; I could tell because their fingers fitted the bruises on my arms exactly. I tried a "Hey guys, what's up?" but they didn't respond. I let myself go meek: no struggle, let them think I'm putty in their hands. The echoes of our own feet closed in round us. We could have been inside a pyramid, the real thing, but for an occasional dim glow of a FIRE EXIT sign.

Ahead, there was a faint sound of voices, oddly like, *exactly* like, the hubbub of a bar. The next door on the left, I guessed. As we came alongside I went limp. Melted out of their grip. Dropped on all fours, twisted sideways and lunged at the door. By luck it opened inwards and it wasn't made of stone. As I burst through the doorway the crowd inside stepped back, freeze-framed in mid-sip or mid-conversation, and I saw the way things were in this most exclusive night club, Nefertiti's Tomb.

Black was the house style; you could say funereal. Not mock-Egyptian, though: these were audience, not actors. Whatever went on, it wasn't dressing-up for grown-ups like the other timeshares. This was a black-tie crowd, dressed like topdoggers do for the Presidential box at Covent Island Multi-Opera – for some special show that was advertised nowhere, would get no reviews, and was going to take place hush-hush, literally underground.

I had a feeling that I might be part of it.

Even if I hadn't been, I was now.

The henchmen must have paused to lay their masks aside, because I had just a moment's grace. Then they were there behind me: "Excuse us, please, ladies and gent. . ." one boomed. As the customers looked up I dived for their legs. They shrank back, some squealed, there was jostling, tut-tuts, protests; drinks worth a week's wage a glass were spilled over me, but a path cleared. I squirmed through, staggering upright . . . almost into the arms of a dead man. He was very brown and shrivelled, and his swaddling bands were crumbling off him, and his head turned sideways almost as if he was shy. Then I saw what he was – a mummy. There were others – a couple of cats, a crocodile even – but he had pride of place, hung on the wall eye to eye with the guests in the interval bar.

Four strong hands clamped me by the shoulders. "The Management apologizes," said the henchman who had been Anubis. "Just a slight hitch with the Final Wish. The ceremony will be commencing shortly." I had a flicker of pallid faces staring – several, especially the men, wore matt-white powder – then I was out in the corridor, feet dragging, hauled without much ceremony to the place where the ceremony, whatever it was, was going to happen.

The Final Wish? Was that me?

A smoulder of torches. There was a low stone door, guarded by a pair of effigies, upright, arms crossed on their chests, hands holding ritual implements, a spear, a flail. They stepped aside smartly and the door crunched open. Blank stone walls again: an antechamber. No, an auditorium, except that there was no stage, no screen, just a rank of black-upholstered virtualizing seats. They bristled with wires and headsets, all the gear for a head-to-toe virtuality experience. Somewhere back up the corridor a soft bell tinged: "Ladies and gentlemen, please take your seats in five minutes. Thank you." Jackal-Head held me as Hawk-Head jerked open another smaller door. As it cracked in place behind us I knew this was it. The Tomb.

I knew a bit about funeral goods but this was a junk shop. In the smoky glimmer I saw heaps of things – a shiny motorbike, a pair of dumbells, racks of glossy clothes on hangers, clothes I seemed to recognize. Who wore sequined waistcoats like that? There were 3-D snapshots, hundreds of them, piled so close they blurred around the edges. As my eyes adjusted, the same face smiled back at me from every one.

There was the old Major-Domo, younger, in happier days. He was plunging out of huge waves on the kind of beach I'd only heard of, with a surf board tucked beneath his arm. He was handsome and grinning. Round him several women gazed, adoring.

There he was, slightly older, with the Prime Executive of Peaktime Timeshares Corporation in person clasping him warmly by the hand. There was a glittering trophy in the form of an elegant figure bent almost double in a formal bow: *Master Major-Domo of the Year, Third Year Running*, said a banner headline floating in the air behind. Then there were dozens of others of the M-D serving drinks, exchanging banter with this, that or the other mega-mega-star.

It was too much. Yes, it *was* too much. He couldn't have met all these people, not in the tatty old Sherbet Fountain. He hadn't won M-D of the Year, not even once, not even reached the hemi-demi-semi-finals, or we'd have never heard the end of it. And the Prime Executive, we all knew, was a fiction, a front for vague boardroom conspiracies that shifted week by week.

It wasn't true.

What I was looking at, in this 3-D photo album, was a catalogue of everything the sad old geezer ever wanted to be. It was an exhibition, a major retrospective of his dreams, all produced as if they'd really happened, ranged in order round that stone plinth in the centre. . .

That stone plinth. It was long and hollow. It was a sarcophagus. I took a step closer. In it, there he was. I realized for the first time: I don't even know his name. What could I call him, but *the ex-M-D*? He was laid out in the kinds of silks and sequins he'd have killed for – not a bald patch or embarrassing stain in sight – and his stubble was perfectly shaved, neat as never before. He looked calm and suave and almost handsome. Only the wires and the electrodes round his head and wrists and ankles spoiled the effect a little.

I was almost sorry for the alligator business, and it occurred to me that I could say so. Sort of out of respect. I took a breath. That's when he spoke to me.

"Scipio," he said, and smiled. "At last. At . . . *last*. . ."

"Do you want him offed now?" said Anubis. "Do you want it quick or slow?"

"No, no. . ." Carefully the M-D levered himself up till he was comfortably reclining. "We'll do this the classic way. Simply seal him in with me."

"Wh—?" Hawk-Head's big hand stopped my question in mid-breath.

"Don't interrupt the Bridegroom Of Isis," he said. "This is his big night."

"In Egypt, of course," the M-D went on as if nothing had happened, "there'd have been hundreds of you. All the Pharoah's servants – cooks, favourite handmaidens, the lot. He'd need them with him in the Afterlife. . ."

"Afterlife?" I shook my head free. "You don't believe all that stuff," I said, "do you?"

The M-D smiled. "Well. . ." he said. "Not in general, no. Think of this more like revenge. That trick of yours with the alligator, that's what did for me. It was all downhill after that. I'd have still been top dog at the Sherbet Fountain if it hadn't been for you."

"Hold it. . ." I started. Hawk-Head clenched his fist.

"On the other hand," said the M-D, "it might *just* be true. In which case you hitch a lift to the Afterlife with me. And I hope you're grateful. Whatever it's like there it's got to be better than this pile of ordure, don't you think?"

There was that melodious *bing!* again, and a soft voice came through. "Excuse me, but the ritual will commence in three minutes."

"Any last requests, sire?" said Anubis. "Do you want the trashtype unconscious?"

"No, no, let him watch. I like to think how jealous he'll be when I'm gone."

The door shut with a tactful groan. It was just him and me.

"Gone?" I said. "Gone! You mean, you're . . . you're really going to. . . ? I mean: how? Why?" I was running out of questions. "Are you ill?"

"Not ill. But finished, everybody knows that. Any

moment I'd have been thrown out in the trash. . ." his nose wrinkled with distaste, ". . .with the likes of you. Then they offered me a deal. The big one. Everything I wanted: food, drink, women. . . Oh yes, Seven Veils is *nothing* compared to. . ." His eyes went dreamy. "All that," he went on, "in exchange for this."

"And what's in it for them?" I said.

"For them? Oh, they get to come with me. Not really, of course. . ." He touched the electrodes wired to his head. "But virtually. And that's real as real. They get to feel it all over, right up to the moment the Ka – that's the soul, in Egyptian – flies out of the body. It's the ultimate trip. Those topdogs who've been everywhere, done everything, they pay big cred for it – big, *big*. . ." The thought of big cred made his eyes shine, even now. "Great invention. And you played a part too, of course. You didn't know? Remember Ivo Maccaby? It was his last broadcast, just as that psycho trucker offed him, that gave Mr Rocco the idea. His great-grandfather made snuff movies. That's where the family fortune came from." He sighed. "But now they want it live – pardon, my little joke. Be honest, trashtype, what could be better? To die happy. Every wish you ever wished . . . granted. Even down to the last little drop of revenge."

I looked round the room, at the snapshots of the perfect life they'd given him. "They've certainly laid on everything," I said. Early pictures: him, young, on some sunny island. In one, the palm trees in the background seemed to have been bending in the wind.

"They've even," I said, "fixed you a little hurricane."

He looked at me. "What?" he said.

"It's true. It's starting now, outside."

"Can't be. Not here..." His voice went faraway. "No... That would be too much to ask – to feel that ... that thrill ... the wind ... to see the trees..."

"You can see them now," I said. "Just step outside."

Bing! The intercom purred. "Prepare to start the ritual."

The M-D was quite still a moment. Then he lay back, slowly. "You always took me for stupid, didn't you?" he said. "Sly beggar."

"It's out there now," I said. "A big black waterspout, I saw it. Coming in off the sea."

Bing! "Prepare to administer the potion." The M-D's hand reached out and clasped a small glass vial.

"Can't you smell it?" I cried. "Can't you feel the pressure building?" The funny thing was, I was almost convincing myself: my eardrums were popping and the air was tingling. "The storm's going to burst, can't you feel it, any moment now?"

"Oh, no," he said. "You don't fool me this time." And he brought the vial to his lips.

There was a thump, and a strange long rumbling tearing sound. The door groaned for a moment, little sprays of water hissed through the cracks, then it fell flat off its hinges and the flood poured in.

From there on it was darkness. The good old stink of Creek water. A gush of it punched me backwards, off my feet; it was waist-deep already, and swirling. Funnelled down the long stone corridor there was a crash – another wave breaking – then a rumble more like a landslide than water as the stuff came sluicing down the corridor. In the antechamber, there was screaming. Some of it might have been the wind. I got hold of a doorpost, as the next wave crashed around me, and I held my breath. Held tight.

Something big was thrashing in the water just behind me, clutching at me, fit to drown. The Major-Domo. Now it came down to it, his body's instincts had taken over; he was fighting to survive. I braced my feet against the door, and heaved him through.

There was a faint blur of light beyond the ante-chamber. Make for it. Something sodden bumped against me, groaning. Everywhere were gargling cries: the audience, still there, maybe stunned or tangled in their wires. "Help!" cried one voice. "Please!" another. "Save me. I can pay, I can pay!" Then the M-D did what I'd never have expected, something that made all our bygones bygones, and I liked him. He threw back his head and laughed.

"You wanna know what dying's like?" he roared. "Have a go at your own!"

The next wave knocked us backwards, jostling with padded seats and bodies, unexplained things floating, maybe debris from the Tomb. On the backwash, I made it out to the corridor. From then on it was only time – hours, nights long, fighting uphill, stumbling and slipping, clawing for a handhold, losing ground, then forging on again, waist-deep, gaining ground again just enough as the underworld filled up behind us, heading for the murky smudge of light that was the portals. And then, when it had been for ever, I was there.

There was a sound of wind like metal tearing. Where there should have been earth there was water. Where the sky should have been, it looked like stone.

A black cloud, low and round as a grindstone, covered Psylicon Beach exactly, leaving just a chink, a smudged glimpse, of the normal day beyond. Belts of rain would come fanning towards me, big drops hitting like stones, so all I could do was crouch down and cover my eyes. When I looked again I'd see the grey blur moving off and in the brief clearing the coil of a waterspout, black as the cloud, swayed centre stage like the M-D's girl-friend in her Seven Veils routine. Fragments of things – chairs, tables, trees, a splintered billboard – dropped from it like dandruff, slowly on to the turbid wash of water where the gardens had been. There they floated, swirling in whirlpools, knocked about by the waves that panned out this way or that, or tugged on currents that eddied in and out of where the streets had been.

Every now and then, above the rip of wind, there would be a dull wet crumple, and the end wall of a block would give way. There was the Freestyle, all its private storeys opened like a doll's house. There was the Pleasure Dome, cast adrift. For a moment I thought it might ride out to sea, a magnificent glittering jellyfish; then it shuddered and turned turtle, just like that, and sank.

The next wave knocked backwards through the portals. As I spluttered and got upright I remembered: that side door. The office. Rocco's console. I barged at it. Locked. "Here..." I yelled as the M-D surfaced by me, and he lent his shoulder. With a wet thump the door burst inwards and we fell floundering across the floor.

Rocco didn't turn round from the console. He must have been knee-deep already, staring at the fingerprint of isobars that filled the screen. I clutched at him. "Switch it off, for God's sake. You said it was under control!"

He turned round slowly. Was there panic on his face? Megalomaniac laughter? Anger? Vengeance? None of that. He looked young, and crushed and helpless, like Chiara had been.

"It was," he said flatly. "Calibrated to the nearest erg and therm. It's a matter of very fine judgment."

"So ... so..." the M-D spluttered, waving at the doorway. "What's all *that* out there?"

"She did it," said Rocco. "Not me. Her... Yes, you know who I mean. Chiara. When my back was turned. While..." For the first time there was a flicker of anger. "While I was dealing with you."

"Her?" I said, dumbly.

"She turned all the dials to Max," he said. "Tipped the balance. Started the process."

"Then stop it..." I burst out, but he shook his head. "You think I haven't tried? No good. We can't control it now." A new surge of water sloshed around us, lapped against the console. There was a little sizzle, and the screen went blank.

"Why?" he said. "What possessed her...?" He was frowning like a little boy whose toy just broke.

"Where is she?" I said. He didn't answer. "Rocco, where's Chiara?"

He shrugged. "Last thing she said was: *I need a breath of fresh air*. She went outside..." I was already at the portals. With the next wave the corridor filled up completely, slowly vomiting a mess of things that floated. The first thing I clutched at was a body in a black suit, but I pushed it away. There was a floating jackal head, then a wooden mummy case. Yes, I clambered on; it didn't quite sink, and I sculled it out on to the flood like any other boat.

* * *

It was the M-D, the next morning, who told me most about that day. It seems I was diving like a madman, wherever the floodwater washed me, here and there and everywhere. I couldn't have seen a thing down in that swirling murk, but I seem to remember glimpses: the poolside bar back at the Sherbet Fountain, underwater now and dreamlike, silent and lost as the old world ruins I dived in for plunder out by the Stacks. I get glimpses of a mermaid face, that smiles and lights up to see me, but that's not a memory, that's just my dream.

There were people down there in the Sherbet Fountain, still sat at their ease in loungers as if nothing had happened, though the alligators were starting to take an interest. I dived again and again to check their faces. None of them was her.

Then it was dark, but I still went on diving till the M-D hauled me on to an island of a building and either he rabbit-punched me or I passed out in his arms. When the daylight came the storm had gone. The sky was blue-white; a heat haze was building. For Psylicon Beach, it was like any other day.

Where the Beach itself had been, there was another coastline. New gullies and creeks had been gouged out, and new sandspits piled into place. Where the timeshares had been was a still-damp, rotten-smelling plain. Bits of buildings, less than the stumps of the Outer Lots, rose through the mud. One day there might be archaeologists who'd come and study this.

Out on the slopes of the hill were huddles of survivors – trashtypes mostly, but there were shivering guests there, looking helpless, trying to fit in. I checked every huddle for Chiara. Asked and asked again.

Out to sea there was nothing left. The Tower and the Stacks were simply gone. Swept away. Rocco would have liked that. Somewhere inland, up that secret gully the Australian had shown us, might be Metanoia, Guppy, Duckhead, Cazzie and their outlaw band. Maybe I'd try to find them. But I couldn't leave the place, not yet.

The mud was baking and cracking in the heat as I paced it. It was getting to midday, in the kind of heat no one in their right mind ventures out in, the glare close to blinding, when I got the sign.

Over there, a wink of red. Then, as I moved my head, it flickered through orange, yellow, green, blue, indigo, violet, gone... Scarcely breathing, I tracked it, pace by pace, till there it was, set like a jewel in the hardening mud. The broken crystal.

I held it in my palm a moment, taking deep breaths, like for the deepest, hardest dive I'd ever done.

Then I slipped it in my bag. My last find. No more deals. No more trinkets. No more Scip, no more little old kid who'd be thirteen for ever. No Psylicon Beach.

It was time to move on.

About the author

Philip Gross is an award-winning poet (for adults and young people) as well as a novelist. He also writes plays and recently, with composer Glyn Evans, a schools' opera, *Snail Dreaming*.

He has two teenage children, lives in Bristol and leads creative writing workshops in schools and at Bath Spa University college.